HER MASTER AT LAST

BJ WANE

Copyright © 2016 by BJ Wane

Published by Stormy Night Publications and Design, LLC.
www.StormyNightPublications.com

Cover design by Korey Mae Johnson
www.koreymaejohnson.com

Images by The Killion Group

All rights reserved.

1st Print Edition. March 2016

ISBN-13: 978-1530456789

ISBN-10: 1530456789

FOR AUDIENCES 18+ ONLY

This book is intended for adults only. Spanking and other sexual activities represented in this book are fantasies only, intended for adults.

CHAPTER ONE

Cursing Jack, Morgan tossed the phone onto the seat as she tightened her grip on the steering wheel with both hands. Why the hell wasn't he answering? Didn't he know she needed him?

The blinding snow rendered visibility impossible, but she had no choice but to keep pushing on. She had never been to Jack's lodge in the Colorado Mountains, so she'd stopped for directions when she'd reached Denver.

Once again, she'd let her rashness get her into trouble, but this time she couldn't get hold of Jack to bail her out. Not heeding the gas station attendant's warning about a snowstorm heading their way hadn't done her any good. She had been sure she could get to Jack's lodge before the weather turned impassable. Shit, was she ever wrong.

Flipping the defroster on high, she slowed to a crawl as she struggled to keep her small BMW on the narrow two-lane road. With no sign of another vehicle since turning off the main highway onto this winding road, an eerie sense of isolation had unease slithering up her spine. Ice-covered trees veiled the rest of the mountain, obscuring her from the world.

According to her instructions, she should only be a few

miles from the secluded Bear Creek Lodge. Why the hell he had to live so far off the main thoroughfare was beyond her, and Jack, who told her everything, had refused to divulge anything about his business.

As usual, she hadn't stopped to think things through. After discovering Joel, her now ex-fiancé, in bed with another woman, and after having a bitter argument with her mother, she had thrown a few things in a bag and left. Her only thought had been to turn to the one person who had ever given a shit about her, and so she'd steered her car toward Colorado and Jack.

Morgan had been just seven years old when she'd first met Jack and he'd spent the summer working the grounds on her parents' estate. At fifteen, he'd been big, hardworking, and gruff, but he was more tolerant of her wayward antics than her parents, who had continued to ignore her no matter what she did to get their attention. By the end of that summer, Morgan had idolized Jack and vowed to marry him some day. That promise had lasted through the next nine months after she returned to boarding school and it had been reinforced every summer over the next several years when she returned home and spent every available minute by his side.

When Jack turned eighteen, he'd joined the Army and had broken her fragile ten-year-old heart. For four years she hadn't seen or heard a word from him. Devastated over his desertion, she'd coped with it much the same way as she had her parents' indifference, by acting out.

With Jack gone, she wasted no time trying to gain her parents' attention and failing with dismal regularity. By the time she turned fourteen and Jack returned from the Army and a tour in the Middle East, Morgan had been expelled from school five times for everything from smoking and drinking to vandalism, and her grades had gone from straight As to Ds.

When Jack returned, he immediately took up residence in their small guest house to work full time on her parents' ten-acre estate as everything from head groundskeeper, plumber, and electrician to all-around handyman. Upon hearing of his return from their cook, Agatha, Morgan flew from the house down to the guest house, calling his name.

She'd never forget her first sight of him standing in the open doorway, a small grin on his face, his arms outstretched as he waited for her. Taking a flying leap, she threw herself into his arms as he enfolded her in a bear hug.

"Hello, princess," he greeted her in his rough voice.

Morgan struggled to swallow past the tight lump lodged in her throat and squeezed her eyes to keep from crying at hearing his nickname for her. "I've missed you, you big jerk!"

"And I've missed you, brat." Grasping her arms, he pulled her away from him and looked down at her. "Look at you, all grown up. What happened to the gangly kid with pigtails and skinned knees who I left?"

Morgan was secretly glad he'd noticed the changes in her. Much to her mother's chagrin, she did not take after her. By the time she reached puberty, she already had a full figure and topped her mother's petite five foot two by four inches. Not knowing how to respond, she pointed out the changes in Jack. "You've changed too, Jack. You're even bigger! What did you do in the military?"

"Nothing suitable for young, impressionable girls to hear. But I am sorely disappointed in you, princess, if what I hear about you is true."

She had never been ashamed of herself until that moment. When all she ever wanted was for someone to love her, it seemed all she could do was disappoint them. "You haven't been back long enough to hear anything," she had laughed to hide her unease.

"Hired help talks, kiddo. You know that. Kicked out of school, failing grades, and in need of an attitude adjustment, according to several sources. Your mom and dad must be fit to be tied."

"My parents couldn't care less about me and you know

it, Jack."

And here she was, she mused, thirteen years later, still running to Jack with her problems and insecurities, still wishing he would quit treating her like a kid sister and see her as a woman instead of that annoying child who followed him everywhere.

For three years, Jack had worked full time for her parents and for three years he had been the one she turned to whenever she needed anything. He never sounded put out with her when she'd call him from school to help her with math, or when she wanted to bitch about the snobs at school she didn't seem to fit in with. He was the one who taught her to drive the summer she turned sixteen and the one who lectured her when she got so many tickets that her parents' insurance threatened to drop her. It was his shoulder she cried on when she got stood up for her first date and his arms she sought comfort in when her parents forgot her birthday. Even though he still treated her as a kid sister, she never quit longing for more. Although they went their separate ways when he moved from Chicago to Denver right after her high school graduation and she went off to college, they kept in touch by email and phone. Over the years she kept waiting, hoping he would ask her to come see him, but he never did.

Now, as she continued to slowly maneuver her car through the snow, Morgan glanced at the silent phone again, praying it would ring. Even when she pissed him off or disappointed him in some way, Jack never stayed angry with her and he always promptly returned her calls. She grew warm as she recalled one night shortly after her high school graduation, the one time she had seen him truly angry with her. Her nipples beaded into tight pinpoints, her pussy dampening as she relived that scene.

Morgan didn't have to sneak into the house even though it was after two a.m. Her parents wouldn't be waiting up for her, even if they were home. She turned eighteen two months ago and they had informed her she was old enough to be responsible for her actions now. Tossing her purse toward the priceless antique table to the left of the massive double front door entrance of the Tomlinson mansion, she giggled when it missed and landed with a loud clunk on the marbled floor. She would have preferred going home with her best friend Tabitha after Tabitha's father picked them up at a party of another friend, but he insisted on bringing her home so her parents wouldn't worry. She would've scoffed at that if alcohol and Jack's return hadn't put her in such a good mood. Morgan hadn't seen him since Christmas break and she knew she wouldn't be able to sleep until she did.

Oblivious to the late hour and not thinking he might be asleep, she ran out the back kitchen door, across the green expanse of lawn, and down to the guest house. It wasn't until she saw the small Volkswagen sitting next to Jack's truck she considered he might not be alone.

Youth and alcohol gave her the courage to move with quiet stealth up to the window where a bright light shone and she could hear a woman pleading for something. Apparently Jack didn't care if anyone saw or heard them as the shade was up and the window open to allow the warm summer breeze in. Peeking over the window sill, Morgan drew in a shocked breath at the sight of a naked, attractive blonde draped over Jack's lap, hands braced on the floor, ass in the air, legs spread and held apart by his large foot.

Morgan gaped, watching him swat her already bright red buttocks, eliciting a gasp from the beet-faced woman. When he moved his hand between her legs and his big finger slid with ease through her drenched folds, her own pussy dampened with need. Unable to pull her gaze away from the erotic sight, she spied on the couple, both awed by the woman's eager response every time Jack smacked her ass and then fingered her pussy, and jealous over his obvious involvement with this woman.

Jack continued alternating his slaps with fingering her

pussy, the woman's squirming backside and the dampness coating her swollen folds obvious signs the heat and pain from the smacks were a huge turn-on. When the blonde screamed as she orgasmed, Morgan couldn't help but cup the front of her jeans, rubbing her clit through the material. Picturing herself in the place of the woman, the thought of him treating her to the same pleasure/pain had her untried pussy clenching in need. She must have made some sound, because before she could duck down out of sight, Jack's dark eyes switched from the wriggling red buttocks over his lap to land on her red face.

"God dammit!" he roared, making her cringe. Knowing it was useless to flee, she stood up and tried to put on a brave face as he came storming out the front door. "What the hell do you think you're doing, Morgan?"

At six foot four and over two hundred pounds, Jack was a big man, but Morgan had never feared him. Still feeling the effects from her heavy drinking, she gave him a cocky smile and sassy reply. "Sheesh, Jack, I didn't know you were a kinky perv."

"That is not funny, princess. What're you doing out here so late?"

Feeling brave even though she had never seen him so angry, Morgan threw her arms around him and then went stock still when she felt his huge erection against her stomach. Looking up into his rigid face, she stated naively, "Jack? I'm eighteen now and…"

"Forget it." Grasping her arms, he pulled her away from him. "You've been drinking and you don't know what you're saying. Come on, I'll take you back up to the house."

A perverse part of her couldn't let it go and just had to egg him on. "Are you going to tuck me in?" she needled him, knowing she shouldn't push him but not caring. She wanted what she wanted, and she wanted Jack.

"Morgan." The dark warning in his tone told her she'd pushed him too far. He only called her by her name when he was really upset with her.

The memory of that night could still warm her. As angry as he had been, the next day he took her to lunch at her favorite restaurant and spent the afternoon goofing off with her, just like he always did on the first day she returned home from school for the summer. Neither of them had mentioned what happened the previous night, but over the years, they had joked about it often.

Shivering against the icy wind buffeting her small car, Morgan reached over to turn up the heat. Swirling snow made visibility and driving almost impossible now, forcing her to slow even more.

The last time Morgan had seen Jack, he had surprised her by attending her college graduation. Her parents, of course, had been somewhere in Europe and couldn't be bothered to interrupt their trip to be there for her, but when she'd glimpsed Jack in the front row, a proud smile on his face, she'd walked across that stage giddy with pleasure.

As she continued to drive, Morgan grabbed her phone off the seat and once again tried calling him. Thankfully, she could still get a signal, but he didn't answer. The snow now fell so heavily she could only inch along and hope she was headed in the right direction.

Just as she glimpsed a cabin amidst the trees and released a sigh of relief, she hit a slick spot. Even though she had barely been creeping along, the car went into a spin and ended up nose down in a snow bank, the passenger side smashed against a tree. Hands shaking, head aching, she began cursing up a storm while trying to back out, but it took just seconds for her to admit she wasn't going anywhere. With the cabin still in sight, she knew she had no choice but to make her way to it and hope someone could get her the rest of the way to Jack's lodge.

• • • • • • •

Thirty minutes later, cold to the bone and soaked to the

skin, Morgan arrived at the cabin, her dress slacks, designer boots, and chic jacket no protection against the elements. There were no lights on, and dismay threatening her composure when she tried the door with frozen fingers and found it locked.

Relief warmed her when she spotted a huge log building several yards away, the front entrance lit up, faint strains of music breaking through the continuing onslaught of the storm. Praying it wasn't further than it appeared, Morgan trudged as fast as the piling, blowing snow would allow. This had to be Jack's lodge, she thought when she made it to the covered entry and grasped the frigid door handle with numb fingers. Blessed heat greeted her as she practically fell inside. Uncontrollable shivering racked her cold body, making her teeth chatter and her eyes water. Glancing around the roughhewn lobby, she wondered why no one was sitting behind the front desk to greet newcomers.

Approaching the desk, Morgan looked for a bell, but couldn't find one. Her damp clothes kept her from gaining enough warmth to thaw out and her need to find Jack urged her forward toward the sound of music and voices coming from behind a pair of closed heavy doors. Unfamiliar sounds broke through her befuddled senses as she inched the door open. Pushing her damp hair out of her face, she peered into a large, dimly lit room. As her eyes adjusted to the surroundings, she stood transfixed in stunned awe and excitement at the tableau in front of her.

About thirty people filled the room, some lounging on plush chairs and sofas, and others kneeling at their feet. A small dance floor was off to her right, but it wasn't the gyrating bodies that held her attention. Instead, her eyes moved to the far end of the cavernous room and landed on a naked woman bound on a cross, a man in tight jeans and tee shirt flicking her beaded nipples with a thin crop. The way the woman thrust her chest out told Morgan she actually wanted to feel that instrument of torture on her sensitive flesh. A few feet from the cross, another naked woman lay tied face down over a padded bench, her cries of ecstasy stating clearly that she was enjoying being fucked by the hefty man behind her.

"Are you okay, sweetie?"

Morgan tried not to gape at the leather-clad woman leading a topless girl by a leash. Like Alice in Wonderland, she wondered if she had just taken a spill into a strange new dimension.

"I'm looking for Jack." Morgan couldn't think of anything else to say.

A small smile tilted the other woman's red lips before she turned and yelled, "Jack! You've got a visitor!"

Jack's brows drew together in a frown as he set the flogger down and switched his attention from the sub chained in front of him to the front of the room where Maggie had called for him. Since his lodge was booked this weekend with a private group of BDSM players and since they'd all arrived, he wasn't expecting anyone else. Still, the hunched, bedraggled figure standing in the doorway looked a little familiar.

Reaching up, he unclipped Sandy's arms from the dangling chain and clasped her shaking, sweat-slick naked body. "I'm sorry, sweetie. I need to see to something. Go to the bar and wait for me there."

"Yes, Master Jack." Sandy looked up at him with adoring eyes before moving off toward the bar that ran the length of the side wall.

Frustrated at the untimely interruption and wondering why someone would be so foolish as to be out in this storm, he headed toward his uninvited guest. As he neared the doors, however, his frustration quickly turned to surprise followed swiftly by anger.

"Morgan?" Disbelief and irritation colored his tone as he recognized the curly sable hair and topaz eyes staring at him in relief.

"Jack! Thank God."

As her eyes filled with tears, he reached out and enfolded

her shivering, damp form. "Thank you, Maggie. I'll take care of this. Could you ask Marc to cover for me?"

"Sure, no problem."

As Maggie led her sub away, Jack ushered his unexpected and unwanted guest back into the lobby, shutting the doors to the playroom behind him. "Morgan, what the hell are you doing here and why are you so wet? You're going to catch your death."

"Jack, I've been trying to call you all day. Why haven't you answered or called me back? You always call me back." Her voice broke on the accusation, her brain still trying to play catch-up with what she'd seen going on in that big room, including finally spotting Jack standing behind a bound, naked woman, a flogger in his hand. That the woman was on the verge of climax had been obvious even from across the room.

"Don't take that tone with me, princess. We've been swamped today with the arrival of this private party as well as the snowstorm. I haven't had time to check my messages. Come on." Grabbing her hand, he dragged her to the wide staircase and pulled her up behind him as they moved to the second story. "You need to get out of those wet clothes before we finish this conversation. How'd you get so wet anyway? What'd you do, walk here?"

"As a matter of fact, yes, right after my car ended up wedged against a tree and stuck in the snow."

Jack stopped abruptly and turned to stare down at her in astonishment and growing anger. "Are you fucking telling me you were out in this storm dressed like that? Did you leave your common sense back in Chicago?"

"Jack Sinclair, don't you yell at me! I've had an awful couple of days and went through hell to get here."

As always, the sight of her golden eyes filling with tears was enough to cool his temper. The minx has been wrapping him around her finger since she was seven years old and it had taken all of his considerable self-control not to let her know that. "Come on," he stated gruffly, tugging on her cold hand again. "Let's get you warm and settled and you can tell me what this latest fiasco of yours is all about."

Morgan let Jack haul her the rest of the way upstairs, with fatigue, hunger, and chills making it easy to let him take over. Instead of a hallway housing separate rooms, she stepped into a spacious, open loft overlooking the lobby below. A huge fireplace bracketed by floor-to-ceiling bookshelves took up one wall. Arranged in a semicircle facing the fireplace and entertainment center, large cream-colored leather sofas stood out against the dark hardwood floors. The vaulted ceilings and floor-to-ceiling windows taking up the adjoining wall made the room look even bigger. A long granite-topped eating bar was the only thing dividing the living room from the kitchen. A gourmet chef would drool over the stainless steel appliances, matching dark blue granite counters and copper pots and pans hanging over the island.

"You live up here?" Morgan asked, loving the look of the place.

"Marc and I do. Come on. Let's get you out of those wet clothes."

Morgan giggled and couldn't resist needling him. "I've been waiting to hear you say that for years."

Jack spun around, pinning her against the wall, his dark eyes glaring down at her. "Don't push me, brat. I'm sorely tempted to give you a spanking. And trust me, you won't enjoy it nearly as much as my date did when you had your nose poked where it didn't belong."

Morgan's heart sped up and her pussy dampened with immediate lust. If he kept tantalizing her with hints of his taste in kinky passions, she wouldn't need a hot bath to warm her up. All she'd need was him. "Are you sure I wouldn't enjoy it?"

Jack clenched his jaw, struggling to get himself under control. The damn minx had no idea what she was pushing for and he refused to risk ruining their relationship by giving in to her. Morgan had always been a spoiled little kid acting out to get attention. When her parents, damn their sorry asses, didn't comply, she had turned her efforts on him. Feeling sorry for the lonely little girl with the haunting topaz eyes, he had taken her under his wing. Having two wonderful, caring, and doting parents, he could never understand why the Tomlinsons refused to show their only child any affection. He would have much preferred growing up in a loving home with little money or amenities to the cold mansion and even colder mother and father Morgan had to endure. All the things their money could buy her weren't worth her neglectful upbringing. If it hadn't been for Agatha, the Tomlinsons' cook, and himself, Morgan wouldn't have had any loving adult influence.

It wasn't until five years ago, when he had surprised her by showing up for her college graduation, he realized she was no longer a child, and the feelings that had started to change the summer of her eighteenth birthday from fondness to lust, had not lessened any with separation and time. Given his lifestyle, and not willing to risk hurting her or losing her, he has been keeping her at arm's length ever since.

Now, looking down into her mischievous face and hearing her tease him, he knew he was in real trouble. Because, like it or not, she would be stuck here for the next few days and he knew the hard-on he was trying to ignore had nothing to do with the light flogging and anticipated fuck he had planned with Sandy.

"Dammit, Morgan, you've made me forget my obligations," he growled, just now remembering ordering Sandy to sit naked at the bar like a good little sub and wait for him to return. "Come on."

Jack pulled her into his room, but gave her no time to look around as he continued across the plush maroon carpet into the bathroom. "Strip," he ordered, dropping her hand and turning to start filling the large Jacuzzi bathtub.

"Huh?" All flirting and teasing aside, Morgan knew she couldn't just drop her sodden clothes in front of him, no matter how badly she wanted to get warm.

Steam billowed up from the faucets as Jack turned and placed his hands on his hips to glare at her. "I said, strip. Now's not the time for modesty. You'll be lucky if you don't wake up with pneumonia tomorrow. I have to check on someone downstairs. Unless you need help, I'll be back in a minute." Turning, he stormed out of the bathroom.

CHAPTER TWO

Morgan shook, her fingers still numb as she struggled with the buttons on her coat and it seemed to take forever before she finally got the last one opened. Slipping it off, she let the coat drop to the tiled floor and went to work on her slacks. The steam made quick work of heating the bathroom and it felt heavenly as she took her time removing the rest of her clothes.

As much as she had longed to have Jack see her as more than a friend or little sister, she would never be comfortable baring herself with casual disregard. She was not slender or petite like her mother, and never would be. Although, at five six, she was a good eight inches shorter than Jack, she was by no means small. Her mother had constantly harped about how she should lose weight because men didn't like girls with such big breasts and hips—which hadn't helped her self-esteem.

With a deep sigh, she sank down into the heated water and then moaned as her chilled skin thawed. Years ago, after trying numerous diets and strenuous exercises to no avail, she had given up on being anything but what she was. Maybe Jack liked soft, full-figured women, she thought as she sank deeper into the tub. Closing her eyes, the memory of the last time she saw him five years ago warmed her even more.

Tossing off her graduation cap, Morgan flew across the aisle and jumped into Jack's open arms. "You came! I can't believe you're here!"

"Now, where else would I be, princess? Is this not an important night for you?"

Trying her best not to melt at the warm, tender look in his dark eyes or read too much into it, she kissed his cheek before taking a reluctant step back. "I had hoped but I rarely see you anymore. When are you going to invite me to Colorado?"

Taking her arm, he steered her through the throng of graduates and guests and out into the warm evening air, telling her, "I made reservations at Angels and Kings. I'm proud of you, Morgan. Whatever you want tonight, it's yours."

His deft avoidance in answering her hurt, but she refused to let it ruin the night. A trendy nightclub located in the Hard Rock Hotel, Angels and Kings was a favorite for dining and dancing. Excited beyond belief to be going there with Jack, she wouldn't let his continued refusal to invite her to his Colorado lodge, where he had moved shortly after she started college, mar the little time she had with him.

Giddy with the pleasure of just being with him, she ordered a ridiculously expensive salmon dinner to go with the bottle of ridiculously expensive Champagne he ordered as soon as they were seated at a quiet corner table.

"So, now what? The world's at your fingertips. What will you do with it?"

"I wish," she snorted. "Dad's insisting I come work for him, and since I have a huge debt to pay off, I'm not in a position to turn down the large salary he offered." Sipping the bubbly Champagne, she tried not to let her undesirable future interfere with her time with Jack.

"They didn't pay for your college?" he asked, frowning, but not surprised.

"No. I needed to learn financial responsibility, they said. I'm sure it was so I'd end up in my current position, forced to take their generous offer. I could apply elsewhere, but a piece of paper doesn't give me experience, and I'd be making peanuts for too long starting at the

bottom of the ladder at some other company. At least dad's giving me the assistant's job in Human Resources, next in line for the head position instead of putting me in the mailroom." She saw his displeasure, but held up a hand to forestall the rant she knew he wanted to vent on her behalf. "Come on, Jack, let's just have fun. Okay?"

"Okay, we'll table my lecture for another time. Finish your salmon and then we'll dance."

He caved, like she knew he would. It was only when she wanted to be included in his everyday life he didn't give in to her now. She didn't know what the big secret was about his new home in Colorado, but no amount of pleading, cajoling, or whining over the phone had gotten him to budge on his refusal to let her come visit him.

His enticing invitation to dance with her had her finishing her meal in haste, and she barely tasted the succulent grilled salmon and vegetables as she anticipated getting physically close to him.

Ten minutes later, he led her onto the small dance floor and when he drew her into his arms with an indulgent smile, Morgan had never been happier. He seemed to like holding her close and she couldn't resist the temptation when he bent to kiss her nose, as he often did, to lean up, turn her head, and let his lips land on hers instead. His low groan sent a thrill through her, his tight arms pulling her close, heating her blood to molten lava. When her pelvis came into contact with his obvious erection, her blood turned to boiling.

With a low, muttered curse against her mouth, he kissed her with deep pressure right there on the dance floor, his tongue making an erotic exploration of her mouth unlike anything she'd felt before. Leaning into him, she tightened her arms around his neck as their bodies swayed to the slow beat surrounding them. Surely he now saw her as a woman and a desirable one at that if the hard cock poking her stomach was any indication, she thought hopefully, her arousal escalating. Anticipating what would come next, of leaving the club with him and finally losing her virginity to the one man she desired above all others, she shuddered with longing in his rock-hard embrace.

Seconds later, he removed her arms and looked down at her with a scowl. "I'm sorry, princess. That shouldn't have happened. Come on, I think it's time I took you home," he said, his words dousing the fiery heat his kiss had evoked with the effectiveness of a cold dunking.

Shock and disappointment had her following him out without protest, his retreat behind a friendly but cool facade more painful than his rejection.

"Are you going to ignore what just happened, Jack?" she asked with her usual bluntness when he pulled up in front of her apartment after a silent drive home.

His heartfelt sigh wasn't lost on her and neither was the significance of his reply. "Nothing happened, Morgan and nothing's going to happen. You need to find a nice young man to date and think about settling down. You're not a kid anymore."

"No, I guess I'm not," she murmured as the finality of his statement registered. Leaning over, she kissed his cheek. "Thank you, Jack. I had a good time tonight."

Morgan rested her head against the small bath pillow, sighing as she recalled getting into her car as soon as Jack had left and driving to another club where she'd known Tabitha was partying. Several hours and drinks later, she lost her virginity to a stranger in the backseat of her car. Since then, she'd tried to get over her infatuation with Jack, but none of the men she'd dated or the two she'd had affairs with stifled her longing for the one man she always wanted.

• • • • • • •

Jack kept quiet as he stood in the doorway and watched the myriad expressions crossing Morgan's face. Head back, eyes closed, she appeared relaxed unless you knew her well, which he did. Her mouth had been soft, lips turned up before her chin tightened and her brows lowered in a frown. Her full, beautiful breasts bobbed in the water, her soft, rounded stomach beckoned his fingers, her hips wide enough to cradle his large frame in comfort. She had the type of body he favored most, full and soft, something he had been more than aware of in the past and done his damnedest to ignore. For now he would continue to ignore her lush temptation and instead get to the root of this unexpected visit.

"What's the frown for, princess?"

With a startled squeal, Morgan sat up with a quick jerk, water sloshing as her arms went across her breasts. "Jack! You could at least wait until I get out. Go away and close the door." She tried to sound indignant, but looking at him lounging nonchalantly against the door, his blond hair a sexy contrast to the dark beard covering his face, her voice came out with that familiar catch and her heart tripped with longing. It was always that way with him.

"No, princess. My house, my rules. What were you thinking about a minute ago?"

Narrowing her eyes at him, she replied with her usual bluntness, "About the one and only time you kissed me, and then left me hanging."

Jack remembered that kiss well, and his reaction to having her lush body plastered against his. She wasn't the only one who had been left hanging that night.

"We need to talk." He needed to keep both their minds off anything sexual until he figured out what was going on with her and what scrape he'd have to bail her out of now. He knew it must be a doozy to have her driving clear from Chicago in the middle of a blizzard to see him. Not that he minded being there for her. He never had and never would. But she'd picked a bad weekend to show up unexpected on his doorstep. The private BDSM party booked months ago would take up most of his time and he had no idea how he would manage his responsibilities as their host and keep her occupied elsewhere.

He tossed one of his flannel shirts on the counter along with a pair of socks. "When you're warm enough, join me in the kitchen. I'll fix you something to eat then you can tell me what scrape you've gotten yourself into."

• • • • • • •

"You always could cook as well as Agatha."

Jack turned from pulling the leftover lasagna from the oven to see Morgan looking cute as a button in his shirt and socks. He hadn't thought ahead when he gave her the shirt, but seeing her in something of his and knowing she was naked, her lush body easily accessible underneath the flannel made her even harder to resist. "Lucky for you. Sit down and tell me what was so important you had to drive all the way here in the middle of a blizzard."

Morgan hopped up on one of the stools at the counter, her mouthwatering when he set a plate of steaming lasagna in front of her along with a glass of tea. Not even the reminder of Joel's betrayal could deter her from diving into Jack's lasagna. "Just a minute." Taking a bite, she closed her eyes, moaning in pleasure.

"Morgan," Jack growled, wondering if she sounded like that when she came. "Last time we talked, you were making plans for your big wedding." And he had gone on a two-day binge Marc had been forced to pull him out of.

Setting down her fork, Morgan sighed and looked up at him leaning against the counter with his muscular arms crossed and dark eyes assessing.

Why couldn't her mother have been as supportive and caring as Jack, she thought as tears welled. Her betrayal had hurt more than Joel's.

"The wedding's off. I refuse to spend my life with a two-timing jerk."

Jack had always been overprotective of Morgan, and the thought of this guy daring to hurt her made him see red. She deserved better than that, someone who would love her unconditionally. "He cheated on you?" he growled, quelling the urge to take her in his arms. He was having enough trouble trying to keep from imagining how her breasts would fill his hands, how her nipples would harden in his mouth as he sucked and bit at those tempting pink buds. But feeling that lush body pressed against him would be dangerous. His libido didn't need any encouragement. It raged out of control well enough on its own.

"I caught him red-handed, fucking some skinny blonde in the same bed he had just fucked me in that morning." Morgan shrugged and took another bite of lasagna before adding, "But that didn't bother me near as much as mom's dictate that I still marry him."

That didn't surprise Jack; her mother had never been supportive of her or indignant on her behalf. After all, why start now? If there were two people who should never have had a child, it was Kathleen and George Tomlinson.

"And why would she want you to do that?" he asked, although he could guess. He was pretty sure the marriage had to have some benefit for her parents, otherwise they wouldn't have given their blessing.

"Something about a merger and keeping both companies in the family. Since Joel and I are both only children, our parents thought the easiest and most fail-proof way to do that would be for us to marry and have kids, thus keeping the company in both families. I ran home after leaving Joel's and mom was there. When I told her the wedding was off, she said…"

Jack frowned when she bit her lip and looked away from him in shame. Over the years he had comforted her more than once when her mother or father said or did something to hurt her feelings. He and Agatha were the only ones she trusted and turned to when their callousness and indifference drove her to tears.

"Don't tell me, let me guess. The bitch said you should be grateful he was willing to marry you. What was it this time? That you're not pretty enough, skinny enough, or smart enough to do any better?"

"Something like that," she muttered, looking away from him.

The way her face reddened in shame made him want to hit something. "Damn it, Morgan, you know better than to listen to her bullshit. And you know better than to let her get to you so badly that you recklessly drive for what, two days, risking your life, just to get away from her."

"But you've always been the one I've run to, Jack. It's not my fault you moved so far away. And, I didn't know about the weather when I left Chicago," she answered in defense.

He narrowed his eyes at her and replied softly, "But you found out about the incoming storm before leaving Denver, didn't you? You had to have stopped for directions up here and I'm sure you were told it wouldn't be safe for a day or two." Her casual shrug, as if her safety was of no consequence, pissed him off more.

"I didn't want to wait. Although, after what I saw downstairs, I now know why you've been so closed-mouthed about this place."

The sparkle in her eyes and her impish grin were much preferable to the shame and sadness she had been showing. "Which is precisely why you shouldn't be here. What am I supposed to do with you for the next few days? This group is booked through Monday and I won't have time to babysit you."

Shoving her plate aside, Morgan hopped off the stool, placed her fists on her hips, and glared at him. "In case you haven't noticed, Jack, I haven't needed a babysitter for quite some time. Something you would have perceived if you weren't so fucking blind."

Arching a dark brow at her language, he stated with a calmness her belligerence threatened, "You, princess, have the uncanny ability to get yourself into trouble on a regular basis, so in that respect, I beg to differ. You do need a babysitter. But you're right. You're all grown up now, and it's time you took responsibility for your actions. I need to get back downstairs. You are to stay up here. Pick one of the rooms on the right side of the hall. You can watch television or go to bed. I'll be late as these parties tend to go on for a while, and then I have to see that everyone gets back to their cabins safely. We'll talk again in the morning."

As he moved past her, she asked with her usual candor, "Are you going to fuck that girl you were whipping?"

"Flogging, not whipping, and that, princess, is none of your business." To avoid grabbing her and showing her just how much he'd rather fuck her, he bent down and kissed her nose then strode back downstairs.

As he entered the club, he spotted Marc, his best friend and business partner, strapping Sandy onto a padded bench. *Perfect*, he thought, as he made his way to them while checking to make sure everyone was happy and things were running smoothly. Everyone present have been guests at the lodge before and were well aware of the strict rules they insisted on. A lot of abuse took place in BDSM clubs, and he and Marc prided themselves on providing this safe and sane getaway for those in the lifestyle.

The lodge made a wide assortment of bondage equipment available to their guests during their stay and the club room offered a catered buffet, limited drinks, and dancing with the evening parties. Fifteen cabins housed their guests year round and, other than the BDSM activities, Marc and he scheduled skiing and snowboarding in the winter and guided hiking tours, boating, fishing, and horseback riding in the summer, accompanied by some outdoor bondage and sex games in the warmer months.

"Everything okay?" Marc asked when Jack reached their station.

"Yeah, for now. I'll explain later. Right now I need to relieve a little frustration."

"Then it's a good thing I have Sandy here all prepped and ready for us, isn't it?"

Jack grinned down at the pretty sub who watched them out of aroused, anxious eyes. Arms strapped at her sides, legs restrained with knees bent and spread wide and another strap across her hips to keep her immobile, left her open and ready to be fucked at both ends.

"What's your safeword, sweetie?" he asked her as he cupped her breast and pinched her nipple.

"Flower, sir," she moaned, trying to shove her breast further into his hand.

"Okay, but since your mouth will be filled with one of our cocks, simply hold up both your thumbs if we become too much for you." Turning to Marc, he lowered his zipper over his aching cock. "You got a preference?"

"I'll take her mouth. You can get a little rougher with her pussy." Marc sent him a knowing grin as he moved to Sandy's head. Lowering the head rest, he gently eased her head back before releasing his own cock.

Jack sheathed himself in a condom and moved between Sandy's spread knees. The bench was the perfect height for this and one of his favorite apparatuses. Running his fingers over Sandy's bare, damp folds, he wondered what Morgan's pussy would look like without the soft brown curls covering it. Damn it, he had to quit thinking like that about her. He was her confidant, protector, and friend. Nothing else, no matter how much she tempted him or how much she thought she wanted more from him. Morgan was too young, too naïve and innocent for what he would demand of her as his lover. And he wasn't willing to risk losing their special bond by introducing her to his lifestyle only to find out it wasn't for her.

Jack watched as Marc leaned over Sandy's face and lowered his cock into her eager mouth. His finger slid easily between her plump folds, her pussy clutching it in a tight vise when he moved to pull back. Whimpering, her mouth working Marc's cock with eager suction, she tried lifting her hips toward him. The telltale evidence of that frustration only added to her need, evident in the way her pussy dampened further, coating his fingers and dripping down to her anus.

"Are you ready for me, sweetie?" At her vigorous nod, which had Marc cursing at the interruption, Jack shoved into her, burying himself balls deep with one thrust. Rubbing her quivering thighs, he proceeded to pound into her, his lust too long denied for him to go slow. Glancing up at Marc he nodded, and they both began moving inside her in tandem. Sandy moaned around the big cock in her mouth, her eyes glazing with her impending orgasm. Jack spread her labia, exposing her engorged clit. As he pressed that red, needy bud down against his pummeling cock, she went off like a firecracker just as Marc released his seed down her throat.

Jack reached up and pinched her nipples as he drove into her once, twice, three more times before he let go, his climax ripping through his balls then exploding into her grasping sheath.

• • • • • • •

It took all of Morgan's willpower not to reach between her thighs and stroke herself to climax as she watched Jack fucking the restrained girl on that bench. Crouched at the side of the bar, she remained unobserved as she spied the goings-on throughout the large room. A different woman now hung suspended where she had first spotted Jack. Another woman lay face down over a padded bench, her naked, reddened buttocks positioned higher than her shoulders. The man behind her gave her two more swats with a round paddle before releasing his cock and thrusting into the willing sub. If her shrieks were any indication, she had been more than ready to climax.

Between the pain and humiliation, Morgan couldn't imagine getting turned on by being spanked. Yet, she couldn't deny watching the different sexual activities going on, most of which included some sort of punishment, had her pussy so wet she could feel her cream dripping down her thighs. When she finally spotted Jack, she had to bite her lip to keep from making any noise that would give away her position.

She wasn't sure what had her blushing, what caused the heavy beat of her heart or her palms to sweat. Maybe it was jealousy over him fucking another woman or excitement at seeing how focused he was on her and her pleasure. She imagined it was her breasts he was cupping, her nipples he pinched, and her pussy he pummeled with his big, hard cock.

Morgan had despaired of Jack ever seeing her as more than the neglected little girl he had befriended for years. His refusal to take things further after her graduation five years ago had hurt, but it had been the way he'd avoided inviting her to visit him here, at his lodge, since then that had driven her to accept Joel's proposal. She'd known Joel didn't love her, that he was just doing what was expected of him, but at the time she hadn't much cared. If she couldn't have Jack, she hadn't cared who she ended up with as long as she wasn't alone. It hadn't been until she saw Joel with Cindy that she'd realized she'd rather be alone than live like her parents had for the next fifty years.

"Well, who do we have here?"

A hard hand grabbed her arm and hauled her up out of her hiding place. Morgan looked up into the amused face of a good-looking man with black hair and brown eyes. "Let me go." Struggling against his grip, she tried to free herself to no avail.

"I don't think so, sweetheart. Who's your dom?"

"Uh? I don't have..."

A grin split his dark face as he pulled her closer. "Then you need one. Come on, I'll be happy to top you tonight."

"Let her go, Jim. She's with me."

Morgan's relief at Jack's timely arrival was short-lived when she looked up into his furious face. "Jack, I..."

"Quiet." Pulling her to his side with a hard arm around her shoulders, he spoke to Jim. "Aren't you here with Karen this weekend?"

"Yeah, I am. I thought I'd reward her with a threesome for being such a good little sub lately." Nodding toward Morgan, he added, "She said she didn't have a dom, so I assumed she was available."

"She's not. As a matter of fact, she's not even supposed to be here." Jack looked down at her with cold eyes. "And now she'll be punished for disobeying my specific orders."

As Jim walked away with a chuckle, Morgan tried to pull away from Jack. "Damn it, Jack, let me go. I'll go back upstairs." Panic started to set in as he grabbed her hand and hauled her over to a vacant sofa.

Sitting down, Jack held her hands in a tight grip, glaring up at her. "I warned you, princess. I told you the time would come when you would have to face the consequences of your actions."

With a jerk, Morgan found herself face down over Jack's hard thighs. She wasn't even allowed the small amount of modesty his shirt gave her as cool air hit her buttocks when he flipped the shirt up, exposing her to the entire room of strangers. Mortified, she screamed and struggled against him to no avail. "Let me up, Jack! I promise I'll stay upstairs, just let me go."

Holding her in place with one arm across her shoulders, Jack swatted one buttock hard, raising a bright red print. "No, and the more you fight me, the worse it'll be for you. Would you rather I strapped you down on one of the spanking benches?"

From what she had seen, the equipment was all at one end of the room, with lights on them and even more people milling about, watching. "No, don't you dare!" Just the thought of having her big butt exposed that way brought tears to her eyes. "Please, Jack, don't."

Jack almost relented at the teary plea in her voice, but hardened his resolve. It was way passed time the little princess grew up. "Ten, Morgan. And quit struggling or I'll add to it." He swatted her again, hard, raising a matching red imprint on the other cheek. She had a beautiful ass, soft and round, her pale skin blushing easily under his hand.

Morgan couldn't stop from crying out with the next swat. Turning her head away so she couldn't see the people walking by, smiling at her predicament, she fought tears as Jack smacked her again and again. He wasn't gentle, and these were anything but erotic love taps, she thought as her ass burned with each blow, his hand large and hard as he covered every inch of her buttocks before moving to the top of her thighs.

Mortification and chagrin turned to shock when he switched from hard smacks to soft, caressing strokes over her abused flesh and she discovered how the pulsing pain had left her wet and more than a little turned on. When he ran his fingers in a light, tantalizing graze over her damp, swollen pussy, she couldn't suppress a low moan of need. The heat in her buttocks had spread to her pussy, much to her embarrassment.

Flipping the shirt down, he turned her over, cradling her in his lap as she buried her red face in his shoulder. She didn't know what embarrassed her more, being spanked in front of people, or getting turned on by both the pain and the humiliation.

Regret settled like a heavy blanket over Jack as he cuddled Morgan's soft body against him. He shouldn't have punished her like that. Knowing she wasn't in the lifestyle should have made him at least consider taking her upstairs and dealing with her in private. But he had been so pissed over her blatant disregard of his orders, he had let his anger overrule any considerations he might have given her. He tightened his arms around her when he felt her tears dampening his shirt and heard the slight hiccup she failed to disguise in his shoulder.

"Shh, princess. It's over now and I've got you," he murmured, her muffled sobs breaking his heart. In all his fantasies of introducing Morgan to his lifestyle, none of them had included starting out by meting out her first punishment in public. His only consolation had been feeling the dampness coating her labia, a sure indication of her arousal, and a positive sign she just might submit to him completely. All too soon, he felt her stiffen in his arms and attempt to pull away from him.

"I want to go back upstairs now."

With a sigh of reluctance, he loosened his arms and allowed her to slip off his lap. "Come on. I'll walk you back up." He breathed a sigh of relief when she took his outstretched hand and followed him docilely out of the room. When they reached the loft, she dropped his hand as if burned and moved away from him, an action that hurt. "Are you all right? I can stay if you need me to."

She turned tear-drenched, accusing eyes up at him. "You didn't have to punish me like a child, in front of everyone."

"And you didn't have to deliberately disobey my instructions. There are reasons for the rules Marc and I enforce around here, and reasons for the rules I give you. You're the one who showed up uninvited and you're the one who will have to adjust to my dictate. Now, get some sleep and I'll try to get you back to Denver tomorrow and put you on a plane back to Chicago."

Regretting her actions, Morgan watched him storm away. She didn't want to leave. There was nothing for her in Chicago. She hated her job in her father's company. Though she started out as an art major in college, her parents had insisted she get her degree in business and she'd agreed, but snuck in a minor in art just to spite them. All she had ever wanted to do was paint. Well, paint and fuck Jack, she amended, the warm soreness encompassing her butt working to keep her lust simmering.

Sighing, she started toward the guest bedroom then made the quick decision to go to Jack's room instead. If he was going to ship her off tomorrow, she would fulfill one of her fantasies about Jack and spend the night in his bed. Of course, that particular fantasy included him in the bed with her, preferably with the two of them spending hours working up a sweat together. But she'd take what she could get and hope the consequences for this rash decision weren't too awful.

CHAPTER THREE

Crawling between the cool sheets, she winced as her shifting movements to get comfortable exacerbated the soreness of her buttocks. Her nipples tightened and her pussy moistened as the soreness brought about an unprecedented need throughout her body, a need she had no desire to fight or ignore. Unbuttoning Jack's shirt, she spread it open and kicked the covers aside. The cool air on her naked skin did nothing to alleviate the heat of her desire and with practiced ease she sought her nipples with one hand and her pussy with the other.

She slid two fingers with unerring ease through her slick folds as she rolled her right nipple between two more. She didn't try to suppress her moans as she slowly explored her damp sheath, finding her g-spot and her clit as she continued to torture one nipple and then the other with pinches and pulls on the tender buds. Bending her knees, she spread her legs wider, thrusting her hips up to meet her pumping digits. Images of herself lying over Jack's lap, her ass bared to a room full of strangers, caused her to gush even more, her juices coating her fingers and dripping down her crack as her undulating body broke out into a sweat. Pretending it was Jack's hands bringing her to orgasm, she thrust against her hand, crying out as her thumb pressed against her swollen clit. Shaking, she let the overpowering climax rip through her, her hands never slowing until the last tremors ceased and her sated body relaxed. Sighing in contentment, she kept her eyes closed as she softened her touches and calmed her strokes over her now sore, reddened nipples while taking a leisurely exploration of her vagina, enjoying the soft, warm, damp feel of her inner walls.

• • • • • • •

Cock in hand, Jack moved away from the doorway before Morgan came to her senses and saw him. Guilt over his leaving after her abrupt introduction into his lifestyle had sent him back upstairs, the sounds of her low moans and high-pitched gasps drawing him to his bedroom. His anger at the way she'd ignored his instructions again evaporated at the sight of her full breasts, tight, reddened nipples, and the wet, pink folds of her pussy.

It took every ounce of willpower he possessed to escape into the hall bathroom instead of joining her on that bed and letting his hard cock replace her fingers. Leaning one hand against the wall above the commode, he jacked off with the other, the image of Morgan's lush body writhing on his bed, her hands busy doing everything he longed to do to her body spurring him on. It only took seconds for him to stroke himself to climax, his fist tightening around his cock as he fought to suppress his groan of pleasure. His orgasm seemed to go on and on, ripping from his balls all the way up his spine, leaving him shaking and making him realize he was in deep shit where Morgan was concerned.

On one hand, he knew it would be best if he packed her off tomorrow. But on the other, now that he had seen her response to her first spanking, how the hell could he send her away without exploring her depths further? Swearing a blue streak, he zipped up his jeans, washed his hands, and quietly left the bathroom. Ever since that girl was seven years old, she had been able to twist him up in knots. He was very much afraid the time has come for him to quit running from her and to confront his feelings and his lust. And that just pissed him off more.

Returning to the club room he saw things were winding down and there were several couples ready to be escorted back to their cabins. Between him and Marc, it took over an hour to make sure everyone got back to their cabins safely and arrangements were made to meet for skiing. The snow fell in a steady flow of large, white flakes, but the wind had died down and tomorrow looked like it could be a great day for the slopes.

"That should take care of everyone," Jack said as he returned to the club room and shrugged out of his snow-covered coat.

"Good, I'm beat," Marc replied from behind the bar as he finished wiping it down. "They were pretty enthusiastic tonight, but, thankfully, there weren't any problems. Had to remind a few of them to loosen some restraints and as always, had to keep an eye on Gary. His eagerness to please is going to land him in trouble one of these days, especially if he gets paired with the wrong domme."

"Yeah, I noticed that." Taking a seat at the bar, Jack nodded his thanks when Marc slid a glass of whiskey to him. Wanting to be alert to any potential problems, neither Marc nor he ever drank until the evening wound down. Limiting everyone else's drinks helped ensure the safety of their BDSM play.

Leaning muscled arms on the bar, Marc asked him, "Want to tell me about the pretty brunette with the nice ass you had over your lap earlier?"

"Morgan." Just her name said it all as Jack knew it would. Even though he'd never met her, Marc knew all about Morgan and Jack's battle to keep their relationship strictly platonic. Friends for years, they knew each other well and had no secrets between them.

"Wow. Your descriptions didn't do her justice. From what I saw, she's a real cutie with a killer body. A lethal combination."

"Tell me about it. And it looks like I'm stuck with her for a few days." Jack downed his drink, wondering if Morgan was asleep yet. He sure as hell wasn't going back upstairs until she was.

Marc's chuckle lacked sympathy. "You've had a hard-on for that girl for years. Don't you think it's time you took care of it?"

Jack scowled at his friend. He and Marc had met in the military and soon discovered their mutual interest in BDSM. Through trial and error, they realized neither one them would be content with vanilla sex. They both enjoyed bondage and doling out occasional mild punishments to wayward subs, neither into any of the extremes the lifestyle could lean toward. Ten years ago, they had both saved enough to open this lodge and were finally able to cater to those who were like-minded. Jack had unburdened himself about the tug-of-war feelings he fought for Morgan over the years and Marc had been a good sounding board.

"I've told you before, Marc, I'm not risking our relationship by fucking her." No matter how much he wanted her.

"Then what kind of relationship do you have? Friendship makes for a cold bed, Jack, especially around here when the days can get long and lonely in the winter. I saw the look on her face when she first spotted you by Sandy. That girl has it bad for you and you'd have to be blind not to see it."

"It's just hero worship. I was there for her when she was a kid and when no one else was. I'm not taking advantage of that."

"Shit, Jack. Pull your head out of your ass." When Jack scowled at him, Marc ignored him and continued. "She's known you for twenty years and she hasn't been a kid for nine of those years. Give her a little credit to know what, and who she wants."

Jack's scowl turned to a smile at his friend. "You got a look at her ass and you want a piece of that. You're not fooling me."

"Well, yeah. Who wouldn't? So, if you don't claim her, I just might while she's here."

"Not without my permission and presence you won't, asshole." Jack knew Marc was just goading him. Marc carried his own hard-on around for a woman and never showed an interest in anyone for longer than a night or two. Besides, he also knew Jack would kill him if he made a move on Morgan.

Walking around the bar, Marc slapped Jack on the back. "Make up your mind, bro. You either want her or you don't. She's here, you're here. Explore a little with her and see where it goes. If it doesn't work out, you've got twenty years of foundation to fall back on. Your friendship will survive."

"Did yours?"

Marc's green eyes flashed with pain before he closed off his expression with a mask of indifference. "We didn't have that bond, the years of friendship, or the trust needed to survive our fallout. That's a mistake I have to live with."

Jack felt bad for causing his friend pain. They had both volunteered to help with a newbie weekend at a friend's club in Omaha last year, but Marc had made the rookie mistake of falling fast and hard for his protégé and pushing her too fast toward a lifestyle she wasn't prepared to fully accept. He'd had to live with a guilty conscience at the way she ran out on him that last night and refused his calls until he was forced to let the whole weekend and her go. Rising, he apologized. "Sorry, Marc. Let's call it a night."

• • • • • • •

Morgan awoke to the smell of coffee and the disappointment of an empty bed. So much for hoping Jack couldn't resist slipping into bed with her and taking her.

Then, considering the slender blonde he had fucked last night, why should he want her when he had women like that available and willing? Sighing, she dragged herself out of bed, took a long hot shower, then slipped Jack's shirt back on before going in search of the big jerk.

Unfortunately, he was nowhere around but his longtime friend Marc was. Morgan had never met Marc personally, but she felt as if she knew him from the way Jack had talked about him over the years. An inch or two shorter than Jack's six foot four, Marc's lean but muscled build, ink black hair, and startling green eyes made him a very attractive man. When he greeted her with a warm, toe-curling smile, she smiled back, hoping for an ally.

"Well, good morning. You're Morgan."

"I am, and you're Marc."

"You're every bit as pretty as Jack said you were. Coffee?" Marc held up the pot, allowing his eyes a leisurely inspection of her from her bare feet on up.

"Uh, yes, thank you. Is Jack up?" Moving behind the counter, she took a seat on the stool and wrapped her hands around the steaming mug Marc set in front of her. "Thank you."

"You're welcome. Jack's checking out your car and retrieving your things. If it's not drivable, we'll find a way to get you to Denver and then back home. The storm's passed so the plows will be out shortly clearing the roads."

Morgan sipped the hot coffee, but it failed to warm her insides. Jack wanted her gone and if he insisted, she'd have no choice but to go home to her lonely apartment and a job she hated.

"By the look on your face, I assume leaving wasn't what you had in mind."

Marc's kind, knowing gaze made her uncomfortable. "I'm that obvious, am I?"

"You wear your heart on your sleeve, darlin'. You want him that bad?" Folding his arms across his chest, Marc leaned against the stove, never taking his eyes off of her.

Morgan found it difficult to look away from his direct, watchful stare. "I've wanted him for as long as I can remember." Sighing, she averted her eyes in embarrassment. "Unfortunately, he only sees the pathetic little girl who pestered him for attention."

Marc's eyes went to her breasts, their fullness obvious even wearing the oversized man's shirt. "Oh, he sees a lot more than you think, Morgan, which is why he's so adamant about keeping you at arm's length. Surely you know that."

He returned the scowl she leveled on him with a nonplussed smile. "I'm not his type," she growled, which just made him chuckle.

"Darlin', you don't know Jack if that's what you think. He likes 'em soft and round, just like you."

"That girl you two were fucking last night wasn't anything like me and he sure seemed to enjoy taking her." Morgan couldn't help the jealous note in her voice and the knowing smirk on Marc's face only made her scowl harder at him.

"Well, Sandy does have a nice little body and is a pleasure to fuck."

Morgan ground her teeth, but then couldn't help grinning at him. "You're a jerk," she retorted.

"I've been called worse. So, while I whip up some breakfast, why don't you tell me what you thought of your first experience in a BDSM club."

"You mean how did I like being tossed over Jack's lap, my big butt bared in front of everyone, and smacked until I was a blubbering mess?"

Marc grinned at her acerbity. "Yeah, how'd you like that? I know I and several other people enjoyed the hell out of it. You have a gorgeous ass, darlin'." Marc laughed outright when she stared at him in disbelief.

"I think you need glasses."

"And I think you've been listening to the wrong people." Pulling eggs and cheese out of the refrigerator, he gave her a 'more' motion with his free hand. "Give. Were you mortified, excited, what?"

Morgan found it easy to lose her modesty and, to some extent, her embarrassment, with Marc. His mild manner and friendly smile made him easy to confide in. "At first I was too shocked to be anything, but it didn't take long for embarrassment to take over. God," she groaned, resting her head against her hand. "It was so humiliating being treated like a wayward child, and in public no less."

Breaking some eggs into a bowl, Marc chuckled at her bowed head, her thick dark hair falling down to hide her bright red face. "Come on, Morgan, admit it. By the time Jack finished smacking that cute little bottom, your pussy was wet."

Morgan raised her head prepared to blast him, but instead found herself giggling at the comical wiggle of his eyebrows. "My butt is not little."

"Your butt is perfectly proportioned with the rest of you. Now answer me."

"What are you making?" she asked instead.

"Omelets and quit stalling or you won't get one."

"Fine," she muttered. "Yes, I was excited, but that doesn't mean the spanking turned me on. It was being half naked with Jack, and just being near him that got me excited."

"You want him that bad, do you?" Pouring the eggs in the pan, Marc watched her closely, waiting for her answer, as was Jack who had just made a quiet return but remained standing behind her, out of her sight.

"For as long as I can remember. If you had ever wanted anyone that bad, for that long, you would understand why I don't want to leave, why I need to at least try to get him to see me as a grown woman who wants more than friendship from him."

Marc shoved aside the image of the young newbie he had taken under his wing for tutoring a year ago on a short trip to Omaha to visit a friend and his new club. He had made a grave mistake with Cassie, one they both had paid for.

Instead of enticing her into his world and getting a chance at expanding on their relationship, he had driven her away by expecting too much too soon. His gaze met Jack's worried look, knowing that was Jack's fear with Morgan. The difference was Jack and Morgan had known each other for twenty years, were already closer than friends and had a special bond, one he believed would withstand a test to see if they could be more to each other than friends, something he knew they both wanted.

Jack must have seen something in his face, because he slowly shook his head as Marc asked, "Tell me, Morgan, how much do you want Jack? You saw what went on downstairs. How far are you willing to go?"

Morgan recalled the total concentration and desire on Jack's face as he had first flogged then fucked that girl last night. To be the recipient of such focused desire would be heady; that it came from Jack would be the dream of a lifetime. "I'd try anything he wanted me to."

"What if you didn't like it, it was too much for you?"

Morgan shrugged as if that outcome would be no big deal. "He'd stop if I asked him to. And I'd always be his friend, no matter what."

Her instinct was spot on and reminded Jack of how well he and Morgan knew each other. The memory of her soft ass warming under his hand and the damp heat of her pussy had kept him awake last night as he fought the urge to join her in his bed and take her. Maybe he ought to take advantage of her unexpected appearance to explore a more physical relationship with her. It wouldn't be the first time he had given in to her, and it certainly wouldn't be the last. Still, he couldn't imagine his life without Morgan in it, a definite risk he would be taking if, in a few days, she ran from him in disillusionment.

"That's good to know, princess," he said, making a quick decision to test her.

Morgan jerked, swiveling around in guilt to see Jack leaning nonchalantly against the back of the sofa, his muscular arms folded across his chest, his dark eyes unreadable. "How long have you been there?" She couldn't prevent the spread of a heated blush over her face even though she glared at him.

"Long enough." Moving toward her, he dropped a kiss on her nose before taking a seat next to her. "Breakfast about ready?" he asked Marc.

"Just about."

Morgan's accusing glare didn't change his unrepentant grin.

"A look like that will get you punished, darlin'," Jack warned.

"You could've told me he was there before I made an idiot of myself," she snapped at Marc, ignoring Jack's threat and the way her nipples tightened and pussy spasmed in reaction to it. Uncomfortable with both men's close scrutiny, she cursed as she squirmed on her seat. One hour in their club room as an observer and one trip over Jack's knee had left her in a state of perpetual need.

"Eat, Morgan, and we'll talk," Jack instructed, using his no-nonsense tone.

After Marc set a plate with a large, fluffy omelet and bacon in front of each of them then took his seat, Morgan worked up the nerve to ask Jack, "Are you going to make me leave?"

"Your car will have to be towed, but I brought your bag with me. You have three choices, princess." Jack looked at Marc, silently seeking his encouragement and support. With his encouraging nod, Jack gave in to the inevitable. "I can drive you back to Denver and put you on a plane back to Chicago, or you can hang out here for a few days while you decide what you want to do about your engagement, agreeing to stay up here while this group is playing in the clubhouse."

Morgan swallowed her bite of eggs with difficulty then sipped her coffee, waiting for her third choice as neither of those appealed to her. When he remained quiet, she tentatively ventured, "And the third choice?"

Setting down his fork, he gave her a direct look. Her pretty topaz eyes stared at him with such hope, such longing, he knew he couldn't deny her or himself any longer. "Or, you can stay here a few days and we'll see if you're really willing to submit to me sexually." Jack's cock hardened, seeing desire and excitement replace the wariness in her eyes, and it took all of his considerable control to keep from grabbing her, bending her over the stool, and fucking her until she screamed in pleasure.

"I choose door number three," she answered before he could change his mind. He was offering her a chance at everything she had ever wanted, she wasn't about to hesitate now.

"You always were rash and impetuous, princess. Let me show you what that will get you around here. Come here."

Morgan followed Jack when he rose, walked into the great room, and stopped in front of one of the sofas.

"Strip."

"Uh?" Morgan's surprise at his abrupt order kept her rooted in place, gaping at him.

Narrowing his eyes at her, he said, "Your only response should be 'Yes, sir.' Do you need me to repeat my order?"

"N-no," she stammered before casting an embarrassed, nervous look at Marc, who had remained leaning against the kitchen counter, watching her closely.

"Never mind Marc. If you want to be with me, you'll have to get used to having him around, as well as public play."

Morgan jerked her gaze back to Jack, relieved to see his eyes soften and the small, one-sided smile on his face that always made her heart turn over. Feeling clumsy, she fumbled with the buttons on his shirt before shrugging it off. Her eyes refused to meet his and her hands clenched into fists to keep from covering herself. As both men stared at her, she had never been more self-conscious of her less than slender figure.

"Look at me, princess." When she blushed and her eyes met his, Jack wanted to rave at her mother for causing her to feel so undesirable because of her full figure. Reaching out, he fondled her breasts, rubbing his palms against her hard little nipples. "I like a full-figured woman, I like soft and plush."

Morgan's mortification swiftly turned to desire as he molded her breasts with his big hands, his palms and then fingers rough on her sensitive nipples. She couldn't keep from whimpering when he took both nipples between his thumbs and forefingers, pinching the tender buds until she gasped at the erotic pain. Grasping his wrists, she leaned into him, pleading, "Jack, please."

Chuckling, he released her breasts, grabbed her hands, and sat on the sofa. "Not yet. Last night you received a spanking as punishment. Now, I'm going to show you how much pleasure you can get from the same act." Before her surprise caused her to pull away, he tugged her wrists, pulling her between his spread knees then over his right leg. With his left foot, he separated her legs and held them apart.

He had moved so fast, Morgan didn't realize what he intended until she found herself once again in a prone position over Jack's lap, her naked ass on display. "Jack, wait..." she gasped, her hands reaching behind her to protect her vulnerable buttocks.

Pushing her hands aside, he landed a hard slap on her right cheek. "Quiet. Either keep your hands out of the way or I'll have Marc come over here and hold them." He couldn't help smiling at how fast she moved her hands.

"I'll be good," she complied. It was bad enough he positioned her facing away from Marc, her spread legs revealing everything to his gaze.

"Good girl," Jack murmured with approval.

Morgan relaxed when he did nothing but fondle her buttocks with one hand and lightly run his fingers between her legs, caressing her dampening folds with the other hand. Enjoying the softer touches, she rested her head on her arms, and it didn't take long for her to become aroused or for Jack to bring her to an elevated peak. In her previous experiences, it had taken a lot more foreplay for her to achieve such a heightened state of arousal. Moaning, she soon forgot Marc's presence as she pushed against his hand, hoping for deeper contact. "Jack, please," she begged before biting her lip.

When the next slap landed, Morgan cried out, more from the shock of arousal than the light sting. Two more light slaps fell before he resumed rubbing the flesh he had just abused. His fingers played over her damp slit again then delved inside her to tease her engorged, swollen clit. As soon as her hips lifted for more, he pulled from her pussy and smacked her again, once, twice, three times, each hit harder than the previous one. Her soft cries revealed her need and confusion as he waged war on her senses, alternating between smacking her buttocks and then fingering her increasingly wetter vagina, his fingers tormenting her needy clit just to the point of climax before retreating again.

When his swats turned hard, landing with repeated precision on her cheeks and accompanied by the thrust of now three fingers, Morgan came apart. Hot, throbbing pain blended with soaring pleasure, the combination driving her higher and higher. Nothing could have prepared her for such an intense experience. Crying, she struggled against the overwhelming onslaught of sensations, but when his thumb rasped over her clit and then pressed against the tender, aching bud, accompanied by the continuing barrage of hard slaps on her sore buttocks, she splintered apart again. Screaming, she let the pleasure engulf her, swamp her senses, and take her to a place she never dreamed imaginable.

"Shh, princess, I've got you." Jack cradled Morgan's shaking body in his arms, her response more than he could have ever hoped for. Marc handed him the small throw off the back of the couch before making a quiet exit. Tucking the blanket around her, he cuddled her close, giving her time to come down from what he suspected were the best orgasms she had ever had. Her tears soaked his shirt as he softly praised her. "You're beautiful when you come, Morgan. I loved seeing your pleasure, hearing you scream with it, feeling you come apart from it."

Morgan looked up at him with wide, dazed eyes. "I've never felt anything so intense, Jack. I'm beginning to think there's something wrong with me. These people, your guests, do they do this all the time?"

Jack smiled at the awe and disbelief in her voice. Naïve she was, but his girl wouldn't let her ignorance keep her in the dark. "Some live the lifestyle twenty-four/seven, but very few. Most of them, including both Marc and me, save the domination/submission for sex only."

"Well, that's good, because if you think I'm going to bow down and scrape to you, you better think again."

Her acerbic tone delighted him, as always, but she did need to learn when to curb it. "However, right now you are naked in my arms and we are starting a sexual relationship, so it's time for you to answer 'yes, sir.' Am I clear?"

"Yes, sir," she answered but couldn't keep a straight face. Giving him a goofy smile, she couldn't help but be ecstatic over lying naked in Jack's arms.

Removing the blanket, Jack gazed down at her body, his hard cock insisting he take the feast before him. "You'll tell me if I do anything that's too much for you, if you're unsure or in too much pain," he stated in a hard tone, his voice implacable. He needed to know she wouldn't hold back in her effort to please him.

"I will, Jack, I promise," Morgan agreed.

Pushing her to her feet, he grabbed her hand and pulled her to his bedroom.

CHAPTER FOUR

"Kneel on the bed, ass up, legs spread, head down."

Morgan crawled onto the bed and got into position, the frantic beating of her heart a mixture of excitement and trepidation. At twenty-seven years old, she'd had a total of three lovers, including her one-night stand on the evening of her graduation when she lost her virginity to a guy she barely knew after Jack rejected her. She had never allowed her fiancé or the guy she had a six-month affair with to take her this way. Way too conscious of her larger than acceptable hips and ass, just the thought of being taken from behind humiliated her. But with Jack, doing his bidding seemed natural and exciting. He said he liked her body, and she refused to let her low self-esteem keep her from experiencing everything she could while here.

Hearing him rummaging in a drawer, she turned her head to see what he was doing. When he walked over to her carrying a few objects that made her cringe, she couldn't prevent her uncertainty from coloring her voice. "Uh, Jack?"

"I will take you in every orifice, Morgan. Do you want to back out now?"

Morgan looked at the plug and tube of ointment with

shock and instant denial rose in her before she took a deep breath to calm herself. He would stop if she asked him to, she reassured herself. "N-no, I don't want to stop."

"Good girl." Jack gripped her pink buttocks, palmed those round globes, and massaged her pliable, warm flesh, enjoying their soft firmness and Morgan's low moans of pleasure. Once she relaxed, he spread her cheeks with his thumbs, feeling her flinch as he exposed her anus. "Relax. If you don't like this, we won't do it. But I insist you try it a few times before you decide." Grabbing the lube, he stuck the nozzle into her tight little hole and squeezed a generous portion into her. When she squeaked and wiggled in shock at the coolness, he slapped her buttock hard. "Be still."

A muffled laugh escaped her as she blurted, "You try being still while having something cold shot up your ass!"

He couldn't help smiling at her tone, which was laced with amused indignity, then slapped her other cheek. "That's why I'm the boss. Remember, the one you agreed to submit to? Have you forgotten already?"

He rubbed over the sore reminders of her spanking, bringing about a quick reply. "No, I'll be still, I promise."

Jack put that promise to the test when he pushed a single finger deep into her rectum in one stroke, allowing her no time to deny his invasion. It only took a few strokes of his finger in her ass to have her moaning and pushing back against him. When she whimpered, clutching the covers in obvious frustration, he inserted two fingers and gave her ass a vigorous finger fuck, not giving her time to deny the pleasure or him.

"Jack, please." Shock over the unaccustomed pleasure of having him in her most private place rippled through her, perspiration dampening her body as she struggled to accept this new, perverse yet exciting experience. If she had known what she had been missing all this time, she would have landed on his doorstep long before this.

"Not yet, Morgan. I chose a large plug. You need to be prepared." Pulling his fingers from her tight orifice, he added one more before continuing with the hard, deep strokes, stretching her unused hole and getting it well lubricated.

Morgan gasped, first in pain then pleasure, when he added another finger. Her rectum felt full, stretched to the maximum, but the indescribable pleasure/pain had her pushing back for more, begging for release. "Please, Jack, I can't stand it."

"What do you need, Morgan?"

His tone demanded honesty and Morgan couldn't hold back her plea, no matter how devastating it made her feel. "Fuck me, Jack. I need you to fuck me."

Her answer came as both a plea and a demand and was exactly what he needed to hear. "I'm going to give you what you want, princess, and God help us both if you're sorry afterwards."

"I won't be, I promise." Morgan didn't care how he did it as long as he put out this fire he started in her. Her need had never been so high, her desire so out of control, her thoughts and body in such chaos.

Jack removed his fingers and inserted the plug with a slow push. He'd chosen a special one for her, one that would vibrate while he took her pussy, the dual stimulation sure to send her skyrocketing. She cried out when it finally slipped inside her, her hips swaying with the unaccustomed fullness and foreign invasion. Before she had time to balk, he covered his aching cock with latex, grabbed her hips, and thrust into her gushing pussy, her sheath clasping him in warm, wet welcome.

"Christ, you're tight," he groaned, thrusting deep, giving her no quarter. She had to learn right at the start he liked his sex hard.

Morgan didn't complain. Fisting her hands even tighter, she met his thrusts with eagerness, the slight discomfort from his large size and the added tightness from the plug soon giving way to nothing but pure, unadulterated pleasure. When a slight vibration started in her ass, rippling along sensitive, untouched nerve endings, she cried out at the explosive impact. When Jack accompanied his hard thrusts with painful slaps to her buttocks, she fell into sensory overload that had her sobbing as she met each of his firm thrusts, the stinging on her cheeks enhancing the ongoing pleasure. She came with an explosion around his pummeling cock, her cries echoing in the room.

Jack tried to restrain himself, but as her velvety walls spasmed in orgasm, clutching his cock over and over again, it was too much. Reaching under her, he pinched her clit between two fingers, milking that tiny bud, coaxing her into giving him more. "Again, Morgan. Let me feel you come on my cock again."

"Yes!" she cried out, unable to resist his demand, her body flying into a million pieces again and again as he continued to pound into her. When she felt him come, felt his cock jerking inside her, she came once more, her entire body shuddering in ecstasy.

Jack disposed of the condom in the bathroom before returning to take Morgan's sated, limp form into his arms. It worried him how right she felt, how much he had enjoyed taking her. Now that he knew the silky feel of her wrapped around his cock, what she sounded like when she came, it would kill him to let her go. Morgan was spoiled, willful, and dogged in her determination when she wanted something from him. And he had only abetted her behavior by giving into her each and every time, including this time.

At first it had been because he had been trying to make up for the neglect she'd suffered from her indifferent parents. Now, it was because it gave him pleasure and eased any anxiety he had when he thought about what she might do if he refused her. The last time he'd turned her down, she'd ended up losing her virginity to a jerk in the backseat of a fucking car. He had found out about that incident from Agatha, in whom Morgan confided almost everything of a personal nature. When Agatha had told him how Morgan had cried in her arms late that night, telling her of Jack's rejection, wondering why no one wanted her, he could have kicked himself for the way he'd bungled that night. He hoped to God he didn't have to kick himself later for succumbing to her pleas.

"You have too many clothes on," Morgan sighed as she cuddled against him.

Kissing her nose, he pulled away from her. "Sorry, princess, but duty calls. Marc and I have to take our guests up to the ski slopes shortly. Did you bring anything warm and waterproof to ski in?"

"No, I just grabbed a few things, got in my car, and left."

Jack frowned down at her. "Did you even let anyone know where you were headed?"

Sitting up, Morgan grabbed the comforter, pulling it around her, her gaze disgruntled. "No, and don't lecture me. After my mother's tirade about how irresponsible and selfish it would be of me to end my engagement over such a petty reason, followed by her usual spiel of how lucky I was to have someone like Joel willing to marry me, my only thought was to get away as fast as I could."

She was mad and hurt, which Jack could understand, but from the insistent peals of her phone coming from her bag, he thought it best if she answered her calls. Tossing her another one of his flannel shirts, he instructed, "Check your phone messages while I go downstairs. We have a small ski shop that should have something for you."

When Jack returned ten minutes later, Morgan was wearing the shirt he had given her and was talking to her mother on the phone.

"Someone I've known for years, mother, and no, I will not tell you anything else." She paused while listening to her mother go on and on about her responsibilities, rolling her eyes in exasperation. "I don't care. Then fire me, I hate that job anyway."

Jack refrained from grabbing the phone and giving Kathleen Tomlinson a piece of his mind, something he had managed to keep from doing all these years. He could literally see the pleasure he wrought from Morgan only moments ago being obliterated by her mother's words, words he knew were calculated to demean her only child, belittle her self-worth so she would cave and do their bidding.

"I'm staying as long as I want, mother. I'll let you know when I'm ready to come home, but no matter when that is, I'm not marrying Joel. You'll just have to get your merger another way."

When tears filled her eyes at whatever her mother said next, Jack stomped over to her, ready to grab the phone. Morgan shook her head and turned away from him. "You do what you have to. But so will I. Goodbye."

"Morgan." Jack reached for her, but she stepped back.

"I'm fine, Jack. Let's go skiing."

She gave him a smile that didn't reach her eyes, but Jack knew a good way to cheer her up. "After a shower and a little grooming."

Grabbing her hand, he pulled her into the bathroom. "Strip," he ordered while reaching into the huge shower to turn on the water.

"I think that's your favorite word," Morgan grumbled, her pleasure from finally having sex with Jack diminished by her conversation with her mother. "What if I don't want to?" She felt justified taking her irritation out on him since he was the one who had insisted she answer her phone, something she had avoided doing for the past twenty-four hours.

Jack raised an eyebrow, stating with soft emphasis, "Then you'll suffer the consequences. Strip, Morgan."

Her body reacted without hesitation to his hardened tone, which just pissed her off more. Crossing her arms over her chest, she glared back at him. She didn't know why she was defying him, especially since she wanted to get naked with him again. As always, her mother's condemnation of any possible attraction she could inspire from a man brought out all her insecurities, making her doubt herself.

Generally, she ignored both her parents when it came to their criticism of her, but not where Jack was concerned. Then, she couldn't seem to shove their hurtful words aside. Nobody's opinion of her mattered more to her than Jack's.

"Go away. I can shower by myself."

Though it wasn't easy, Jack ignored the pain and doubt reflected in her whiskey eyes. Now was not the time to coddle her. Before she could grasp his intentions, he had her bent over the counter, one arm holding her shoulders down, the other flipping up his shirt and descending hard and fast on her tender buttocks.

"I expect you to obey me when I give you an order, Morgan." Two swats landed on her ass, raising an instant red hue. "And to trust me not only with your body, but your feelings."

Morgan cursed and struggled against his hold even as lust spiked quick and hot with each smack of his hand. Her position heightened her vulnerability, but having her bare ass as the sole object of his attention excited her, the two combined sensations leaving her shaking with both humiliation and need. With a few well-placed smacks, he elicited a burning pain encompassing her whole backside, one that bled into pleasure so fast it made her head spin. Her pussy grew damp with embarrassing arousal and her struggles soon ceased, replaced by the involuntary lifting of her hips for each well placed erotic slap. Her curses switched to moans, her gasps of pain to whimpers of pleasure.

"I'm sorry. Stop, please… I'll do as you say." *And hopefully get another mind-blowing orgasm as a reward.*

Jack lifted her up and turned her toward him. Holding her shoulders, he glared down at her pink, tear-streaked face. "Do you trust me, princess?"

"You know I do."

"Then from now on, regardless of what anyone says to you or about you, trust that I like and care about you just as you are. I wouldn't change a thing about you."

Morgan knew Jack wouldn't lie to her or sugarcoat his

feelings to spare hers, yet it had only taken a few choice words from her mother to resurrect her insecurities about her body and her appeal. With a forceful, mental shove, she pushed all negative thoughts aside and smiled up at him. "Okay."

She had given in too easily, but Jack let the matter go for now. Morgan was a work in progress, but he was sure the end result of building her confidence up would be worth the trial of obtaining that worthy goal. Unbuttoning the shirt, he slipped it off and nudged her into the shower with a hand on her warm, red butt. "In you go."

Morgan stood under the spray and let the heated water cascade over her head and down her body. Stepping in with her, he grabbed the soap and ran his hands over all her lush, wet curves. She moaned, leaned against the wall, and spread her legs without coaxing from him. He smiled at the look of raw carnality on her face, the utter lack of modesty as she thrust against his hand. Soon he would show her the pleasure to be wrought by having those hips securely strapped down, unable to move while he drove her to inexplicable heights over and over.

After soaping her soft brown curls, he lifted her left leg onto the small seat next to her and instructed, "Stay just like that."

"What are you doing?" She watched him with a wary gaze as he grabbed a razor off the small ledge that held the shampoo and soap.

"Haven't you ever shaved down here?" He tugged her pubic curls as he squatted in front of her then grinned at the consternation on her face.

"No, of course not. Why would I?"

"I'll show you why when I'm through. Now, hold real still. I don't want to hurt you. That could put a damper on our fun for a while. You wouldn't want that, now would you?"

Shaking her head, Morgan watched him as he completely denuded her of all pubic hair. Even though she had always kept it trimmed, the new sensations she could feel as he bared her flesh to his gaze and fingers astonished her. He was very thorough, pulling her lips to the side and gliding all the way down to her anus. When finished, he grabbed the showerhead and directed it over her pussy, making her gasp as the warm water hit bare, sensitive flesh. When his fingers joined the water in caressing her soft folds, she closed her eyes against the onslaught of new sensations. She could feel every small touch, each caress of his blunt fingers as he stroked flesh never exposed before, using his thumbs to open her fully to his gaze.

"What a pretty pussy, all swollen and wet, ready for me. Turn the water away and watch me, Morgan."

Morgan gazed down at him, unable to refuse the demand in his voice. With tormenting slowness, he ran his tongue up her slit, his thumbs keeping her open as he lapped at her. His soft beard brushed her inner thighs, the slight prickles adding to the pleasure of his mouth as his tongue caressed her inner walls, his fingers moving as he stroked her. She couldn't keep from clasping his head and pushing further into his face. His chuckle vibrated through her sheath, making her thrust against his mouth harder, praying for a deeper, harder touch.

Jack pulled away from his succulent feast and looked up at her red, needy face. "Do you like having a bare pussy, Morgan?"

"God, yes, what's there not to like? But dammit, Jack, I need to come."

Jack was pleased to see the sad, haunted look her mother had put in Morgan's eyes replaced by frustrated, unfulfilled need. Throughout the years he'd had plenty of practice erasing that look from her face, but none were as pleasant as his current method. "You sure are a demanding little sub."

Her brows drew down in a frown. "Is that what I am, your submissive?"

"You, princess, are my everything, including my sub. Put

your hands on your breasts, play with your nipples for me. I enjoyed watching you last night. I haven't come that hard from jacking off since I was a twelve."

If she hadn't needed to get off in the worst way, Morgan would have laid into him for spying on her. As it was, the fact he had seen and watched her at her most vulnerable only turned her on more. Despite the blush heating her face, she smiled down at him. "You're bad, Jack, very bad." Her eyes on his, she cupped her breasts in her palms, lifting and squeezing her pliant flesh just the way she liked.

Jack never took his eyes from the sight of her caressing her breasts as he bent his head to taste the succulent flesh between her thighs again. With a voracious appetite, he lapped at her pussy, his lips, tongue, and fingers covering every inch of her bare, wet, soft flesh. In moments she was gasping and thrusting against his face. As his thumb rasped against her clit and his fingers stroked her while his tongue lapped her, seconds later she exploded against his mouth. Her juices coated his tongue and his fingers, her cries rang in his ears, and her body trembled above him as she came apart again and again.

Just when she thought she couldn't take any more, Jack grabbed her buttocks in a tight grip, held her to his face, and set his mouth over her aching swollen clit. With teeth and tongue torturing that sensitive bud, hard hands gripping her sore ass, and her fingers pinching her nipples, Morgan exploded in another climax so fast and so strong it drove the breath from her body.

Without giving her a chance to recover, Jack rose to his feet, turned the showerhead until water cascaded over both their shoulders, then gripped her ass again. "Put your legs around me," he demanded, his voice rough as he lifted and rammed his cock into her still spasming sheath in one smooth move.

She obeyed without hesitation, wrapping her legs around his pistoning hips, her arms tight around his shoulders, holding onto him as he hammered into her. The warm water running between them assisted in allowing their bodies to move smoothly together as he took her against the wall, his cock huge and hard as he moved with ruthless intensity inside her. The hairs on his chest grazed against her sensitive nipples, and when he finally, finally bent his head to take her mouth in a scorching kiss, his beard rubbed against her face, heightening her pleasure. Moaning into his mouth, she accepted his tongue, tasting herself as she savored her first real kiss from him. She didn't know which she found more erotic, the way his lips took her mouth or the way his cock took her body. The two together were an irresistible combination causing electrical currents to sizzle through her veins, a forewarning to another impending, mind-blowing orgasm.

Jack reluctantly pulled his mouth away from hers with a low groan. "Christ, what you do to me. Hold on," was all he managed as he exploded inside her, unable to stop from pounding into her over and over as his release erupted from his balls, up his cock, and into her clasping womb.

As Jack lowered her, Morgan gave him a tight hug. "Remind me never to argue about showering with you again."

Grabbing a large, warm towel, he dried her off with brisk movements before lifting her and plopping her on the bathroom counter. "Stay there a minute." Wrapping another towel around his waist, he went into the bedroom and returned with a small package.

"What's that?" Curious, Morgan watched him open it and remove a small plastic device. His teeth were startling white against his dark beard when he grinned at her, a grin she didn't trust.

"It's called a bullet. Trust me, princess, you'll like this."

"Someone told me once never to trust a guy when he said 'trust me.'"

"I meant other guys, and you know it, just as you know you can always trust me with anything. Now, lean back and spread your legs."

Morgan did as instructed, her look wary as she watched him lift her feet and prop them on the counter. Spreading her knees wide, arousal spiked again, stunning her. She had never been able to get aroused so fast nor so often in such a short time. Nor had her orgasms ever come close to what she experienced with Jack. She either really got off on this kinky stuff, Jack or both. As he spread her labia and inserted the small round object, she decided it was mostly Jack. She couldn't imagine allowing anyone else to do this to her with the same ease and the same lust-inspiring results.

Jack smiled at the consternation on her expressive face. Between the dampness seeping from her pretty pussy, her flushed face, and her heavy breathing, he knew she liked having him teach her new things. Pulling out some bondage tape, he attached the small control box to her side before lowering her legs and lifting her down.

"There. All set for some fun on the slopes. I'll put a snowsuit and jacket on the bed for you. Slip my shirt on first and a pair of my socks. Really, Morgan. I looked in your bag. What were you thinking, coming up here in the middle of winter and packing nothing but a pair of jeans and a few tops?"

"Can we discuss my piss-poor packing later? I want to know what this thing is you have shoved in me."

Kissing her nose, he nudged her out of the bathroom with a hand on her ass. "I'll show you in a little while. Marc already has some of our guests on the ski slopes. I need to see if he needs my help. Get a move on."

Fifteen minutes later Morgan sat bundled in Jack's Tahoe enjoying the view as he skillfully maneuvered the four-wheel drive the few miles to the ski lifts and slopes. The bright sun had chased away all the clouds and shone against the pristine whiteness of the landscape. Now that she wasn't fighting blustery north winds and blinding, blowing snow, she could appreciate the beauty of the mountains. Though the temperature remained frigidly cold, the bright blue snowsuit Jack had selected for her along with the boots, gloves, and attached hood, kept her plenty warm. The soft, pulsing vibrations starting up in her pussy spread that warmth even further.

"Jack," she gasped. "What are you doing?"

"I thought you wanted to know what the bullet does. That's just the first setting, enough to let you know it's there, not quite enough to get you off."

Glaring at him, it took all her willpower not to shift against the seat or rub herself to ease the ache of unfulfilled lust. This was nothing short of torture. "Dammit, turn it off, you sadistic bastard."

"Now, princess, is that any way to talk to the man who spent the morning giving you numerous mind-blowing orgasms?" God, he loved her open expressions, enthusiasms, and frustrations. With Morgan, he would never have to wonder if something was too much or too little. She had no problem expressing herself.

"I'm going to give you a mind-blowing smack if you don't stop that thing. Please, Jack," she pleaded, trying to ignore the way her pussy clutched the small plastic torture device, attempting to coax it into giving her more stimulation.

Reaching into his pocket, he switched it off with the remote. He didn't want to frustrate her too much; at least, not yet. "Better?"

Morgan let out a relieved sigh. "Yes, thank you."

Marc saw Jack pull in and strode over to greet him, masking his envy. Having known Jack for over fifteen years, since their Army days, he well knew of his fondness for Morgan and the war he had waged within himself since returning from her college graduation. He knew of the love he had for first the young, neglected girl, then the insecure young woman, and the battle of keeping her at arm's length he was losing. He knew all too well how the best of intentions could backfire when lust interfered, how those feelings could quickly change when one couldn't accept the demanding lifestyle of a dominant lover.

Jack and Morgan got out of his Tahoe and Marc knew just by looking at them they had spent the past few hours exploring some of Jack's preferences in the bedroom. From the look of stunned, sated pleasure on Morgan's pretty face, he'd say she had no problem with whatever Jack had dished out. Recalling the look of her draped over Jack's lap, her round, soft buttocks lifting for the feel of Jack's hand, the wetness of her pussy evident between her splayed legs, he was pretty sure she had accepted everything else he had heaped upon her with equal ardor and enthusiasm.

"Nice of you to join us," Marc greeted Jack.

"Sorry, man. Time got away from me. I'll take over if you want." Jack felt bad about leaving his friend and partner to see to their guests alone. "Any problems?"

"No, and I'm just giving you a hard time. This group has been here enough times they know the ropes and the rules. Jeff's up on the slopes answering questions and giving pointers to those with little or no experience. We have two of the Arctic Cats out, the rest on skis."

"Okay. We'll ride up and help Jeff then I want to take Morgan out on one of the Cats."

"What's that?" Morgan asked.

Marc smiled at her. She looked cute all bundled up with only her face showing, her nose pink with the cold. "They're snowmobiles. We have five two-seaters and a few one-seaters. They're built for smooth riding, but they're fast nonetheless."

"Boys and their toys," she quipped with a grin.

"You like the toy you're wearing now, Morgan, don't deny it," Jack teased her, referring to the small vibrator nestled inside her pussy.

"Jack!" she hissed, mortified Marc might know what he's referring to.

Marc looked at Jack and when he simply said 'bullet,' Marc chuckled at Morgan's reaction. "Considering what I saw this morning, darlin', knowing you have that little toy tucked inside you is nothing. Are you enjoying yourself?"

Morgan glared up at Jack. "He's as insufferable as you. I want to go skiing now."

"Now that's the Morgan Jack has described to me over the years. She's pouting, Jack. You'd better let her have some fun so she'll be more malleable tonight."

"What's tonight?" she asked the two grinning loons.

"Come on. Ignore him, he's just jealous and wants to cause trouble."

Thinking he was right, Marc watched Jack swing an arm around Morgan and lead her to the lifts that would take them up to the slopes and snowmobiling trails. Yes, he was jealous. There seemed to be a good chance this would work out for Jack and Morgan, and he couldn't be happier for them. He would have liked the chance to explore the strong feelings he had for Cassie last year, but he blew his chance with her through sheer arrogance and stupidity. He knew Jack would proceed with more caution with Morgan than he had with Cassie.

CHAPTER FIVE

"Are you ready?" Jack asked Morgan after he lowered the safety bar on the lift chair and they started their ascent.

Swinging her legs and looking down as they lifted off, she asked, "For what?"

"This." Jack flipped the remote to the vibrator on high, sending Morgan into instant arousal.

With a startled shriek, Morgan clutched the safety bar in her gloved hands as the small gadget vibrated with strong pulsations inside her. Feeling it nestled right next to her clit, she could do nothing but go with the flow and ride out the instantaneous pleasure. Burying her face in Jack's shoulder, she groaned in sheer frustration, pressing her legs tightly together, hoping that would either ease her arousal or send it over.

"Let go, Morgan. Go flying, right here, right now, while we're up in the air. Don't worry, I'll be here to catch you."

It was too much. The dizzying height their lift had taken them, Jack's deep voice, and that insistent vibration between her legs all combined to throw her into a shattering climax that left her breathless and limp with pleasure. By the time they reached the top, Jack had turned it off and her shaking was reduced to small tremors.

"Don't worry, princess," Jack chuckled as he helped her down. "We were too far away for anyone to notice anything." He wondered how long it would take her to lose enough modesty so she could climax and not care who knew or saw. While he found her embarrassment and shyness cute, he looked forward to the day she'd let go without giving a damn who was around to see.

After introducing her to Jeff, a young ski instructor who donated time to these groups in exchange for free use of the lodge's facilities for him and his girlfriend, he outfitted Morgan with skis. "I'm going to relieve Jeff for a spell, but you go ahead and have fun. The slopes are marked as to degree of difficulty: beginner, intermediate, and experienced. I know you've skied before, but it might be best to start slow and work your way up."

"Always protective, aren't you, Jack?" Morgan asked, secretly pleased he hadn't stopped looking out for her even though she was no longer that pathetic, ignored little girl he had first met.

"You're my responsibility while you're here. And I take my responsibilities seriously. Go, I'll join you shortly."

An hour later, Morgan was tired and cold, but exhilarated in a way she didn't think she had ever been. Up here, away from her boring tedious job and from her parents' negative influence, she could relax and be herself. Huddled in front of an outdoor wood stove, she warmed herself as she took in the breathtaking view of the snow-topped mountains from the elevated height. Icicles hung like teardrop diamonds from trees with a glimpse of greenery peeking out here and there. The different views of the mountains and the valley below from the ski lift and then the slopes had her longing for her pencils, aching to imprint the stunning vistas on paper. It had been years since she'd sketched or painted, and she'd missed the challenge of putting her creative juices to work.

Jack had always encouraged her art, buying her several art kits and supplies over the years. Her apartment held some of her paintings and she had sketch pads filled with drawings she'd always promised herself she'd paint someday. Life would be perfect if she could remain up here with Jack, spending her days drawing and painting and having sex. She just had to prove to him how much she wanted him and convince him to let her stay.

"Pretty, isn't it?"

Morgan turned from the fire to smile up at Jack. His brown eyes were warm and his dark blond hair shone brightly in the sun, accentuating the contrast with his dark beard. "Yes," she answered, referring to the deep valley. "It makes me want to draw again."

Jack frowned down at her. "Tell me you haven't given up on your art. I've asked you several times if you were still drawing and you assured me you were."

"When I have time, I play with it. But I've never pursued it seriously, you know that. I have to make a living, and painting won't pay the bills. Just because my parents have money doesn't mean they'll support me."

"No, and you wouldn't want them to. But that doesn't mean you can't pursue a career in art or look for a position in that field. You told me you had paid off your college debts last year."

Morgan smiled with mockery. "Can you imagine mother's reaction if I told her I was going to teach art classes? She'd die of embarrassment right after she disowned me."

Jack shrugged as if her mother's opinion was of no consequence. "So what. Let her disown you. At least you'd be doing something you want to do instead of what they want you to do. You broke off your engagement. You don't have any attachments or obligations to keep you from pursuing another career, this time one of your choosing."

Just the thought of someday being able to quit her job at her father's company and spend her time doing what she loved gave her a heady feeling. "You really think I'm good enough to teach or sell my work?"

HER MASTER AT LAST

For twenty years Jack had been trying to bolster Morgan's self-confidence, trying to undo and countermand the damage her negative, indifferent parents had wrought on their daughter. Sometimes he wondered if he was fighting a losing battle. In the past five years, ever since her college graduation, he had made sure he kept his contact with Morgan long distance. Phone calls and email were all they had shared in his attempt to give her a chance to find her own way, attain her own goals and grow as an independent, self-assured woman. He could see now that not helping her get out from under her parents' control was a mistake. As long as she was around them, she'd never build up enough confidence in herself to challenge herself.

"I wouldn't have encouraged you all these years if I didn't think you had potential to be successful. When have I ever been anything but honest with you? Come on, let's get a hot chocolate then I want to take you for a spin on one of the Cats. You'll love it. You have a few days to think about what you want to do when you get home."

He led her into the courtesy building, which held the restrooms and a small kitchen stocked with hot drinks and snacks. The caterer they used for the lodge kept this place supplied with refreshments as well and he was relieved to find they had made it up here this morning after the storm yesterday. Along with coffee, tea, and hot chocolate, there were sandwiches, a huge pot of steaming hot chicken noodle soup and several kinds of cookies.

After finishing their hot drinks and soup, Jack led her back outside and over to a big garage where they housed the snowmobiles. There was only one two-seater not being used, and he helped her onto the backseat before straddling the front. "Hold onto me, Morgan. We'll start slow until you get used to it. When I turn, lean into the turn. Got it?"

"Got it." Morgan grabbed Jack around his waist, grateful for his big body as he started up the Cat and they left the garage. Once out in the open, he picked up speed, hollered "Hold on!" and let the machine fly. Her screech rent the air as the cold air whipped around them, urging her to snuggle closer against Jack's back. When she felt the vibrations start up again in her pussy, she welcomed the distraction and the heat.

Jack cast a swift look behind him, asking, "More?"

Morgan could only nod her head as the vibrations from the snowmobile underneath her and Jack's hard body in front of her added to the stimulating pulses filling her pussy. As he guided them with smooth expertise over small slopes, around trees, and across the snow-covered ground, the small vibrator picked up speed and intensity, throwing her into a maelstrom of sensations. Rubbing her crotch against the seat and as close to Jack as possible, she was soon screaming out a climax that drove away the cold and left her shaken. Pleasure still whipped through her body, small aftershocks of coming completing apart in ecstasy, when he slowed down and brought them back to the garage.

Morgan's legs wobbled when Jack helped her off and his knowing smirk didn't make matters any better. "I swear, Jack, I've come more in the last twenty-four hours than I have in the last ten years. Had I known about all these little tricks you like to practice, I would've shown up on your doorstep ages ago."

Pulling her into his arms, he kissed her hard and long before saying, "There's more, princess, if you're brave enough and trust me to take care of you."

"I've always trusted you, Jack."

• • • • • • •

Morgan sat in front of the floor-to-ceiling windows in Jack and Marc's loft, her sketch pad in her lap and her eyes on the pristine view in front of her. For as far as she could see, snow-covered mountains and trees blanketed by blue sky stretched out before her. Dressed again in one of Jack's shirts and a pair of his socks, kept warm by the blazing fire he had started when they returned from the slopes, she was more relaxed and content than she ever remembered feeling. She didn't know how much credit went to being away from Chicago, Joel, and her parents' expectations of her, or to being with Jack again and having her long-awaited dream of crossing the bridge from just friends to lovers realized. Either way, she would bask in this feeling for as long as it lasted.

Thus far, Jack seemed happy to have her around and pleased with her sexual responses. Now, if only she knew how to keep him that way. Twenty-four hours in his presence, less than that since they had become lovers, and already she couldn't imagine returning to her staid existence and the bland sex she had experienced. If this didn't work out with Jack, she didn't know what she'd do. She couldn't imagine lying over another man's lap to be spanked and finger-fucked until she was writhing and screaming in climax or allowing another to insert a vibrator and get her off while whipping around on a snowmobile. Recalling that feeling of all-encompassing pleasure enveloping her as she went flying on the Cat made her smile and tighten her legs, squeezing her now empty pussy.

"What're you drawing there, princess?" Jack asked as he came up behind her and rested his hands on her sun-warmed shoulders.

Engrossed in reliving the ecstasy of the past few hours, she hadn't heard him return to the loft. Smiling up at him, she lifted the sketch pad, hoping her thoughts didn't show on her face. "What do you think? I love this view and thought you might like a painting of it. Of course, it won't compare to the real thing, but…"

"I think if the painting is half as good as that sketch, it'll be stunning. Now tell me what you were thinking about. You had a pleased smile on those pretty lips when I walked in."

Morgan turned her attention back to the window, hoping he would think it was the warmth from the fireplace and the sun shining on her face that brought on her blush.

"Just thinking about the last few days and all the changes in my life."

Jack kneaded her shoulders, his dark eyes shifting from the top of her head to look at the view he often took for granted. "Am I moving too fast for you, Morgan?" He had put her through the wringer this morning and already he was planning on taking her again before they went downstairs to join his guests in the club room. Although he would refrain from taking her in public tonight, he did plan to scene with her, a scene that included Marc. Maybe he should alter his plans, he thought when she turned a panicked look of denial up at him.

"No! Jack, don't you dare think about backing off when we've just started."

"Easy. You're new to all this and this is a turn in our relationship we've both either fought or avoided for years. It would be prudent on my part, being older and wiser," he grinned in mockery, "to make sure I don't push you too far too fast."

Jumping up from her chair, she turned to glare up at him. "You're the one who fought and avoided this for years, not me. I've waited a long time for a chance to be more than just your friend, and I don't want to slow down. In fact, if you sped up my education it wouldn't bother me in the least."

Damn her, didn't she realize what a challenge like that could do to a dominant such as him? Maybe he ought to show her, he thought, as he recalled the sound of her hoarse voice crying out behind him on the snowmobile. "Is that so? I think you've gotten a little too warm sitting here in front of the fireplace and the sun, princess." Grabbing her hand, he pulled her into the kitchen, instructing, "Strip."

Morgan knew better than to question him or balk at his order. Although she was a little worried about what he had planned, especially when she saw him put a few ice cubes in a glass before turning back to her, she quickly divested herself of his shirt. Her nipples beaded into stiff points when he walked back over to where she stood by the island counter, his eyes hot on her breasts.

"Very good. No backtalk, I like that."

"Um, Jack..."

"Sir, or master."

Morgan's brows furrowed in a frown at his order. "What?"

"You heard me. When we're having sex, which we will be shortly, you'll address me properly, whether we're up here, downstairs, outside, or wherever we happen to be." Gripping her arm, he ran the cold ice-filled glass over her right nipple, enjoying the sight of it puckering into an even tighter bud and the sound of her startled squeal.

"Shit! That's frigid, Ja..." At his glare she quickly said, "Sir."

Ignoring her complaint, Jack turned her and pushed her over the counter. "Rest on your elbows and don't move from there." With his foot, he pushed her legs further apart until he had a clear view of her already damp sheath. Leaning over her, he set the glass on the counter before plucking two ice cubes from it. "I'll keep you warm on this side, how's that," he murmured in her ear as he reached under her and ran the ice over her nipples, her dangling breasts making it easy to concentrate on tormenting just those enticing buds.

Morgan gasped as her nipples grew numb, the heat from Jack's body behind her an erotic contrast. His jean-clad legs molded against her naked ones, his hips pressed to hers, the thermal shirt covering his hard chest against her back warm and heavy. His arms enclosed around her as he tormented her nipples with the frigid cubes until they were numb. When he lifted away from her, she moaned at the loss of his heat then cried out when his hand landed sharply on her ass.

"This is another way to warm you up, princess." Dropping the ice, Jack caressed her stiff, ice-cold nipples as he continued to smack her bottom, using both hands to warm her.

Sharp needles of pain heralded the return circulation to her nipples, her ass warming from Jack's precise sharp slaps. Their initial sting soon turned to heated pleasure as he tormented her body with masterful expertise. As the painful throbbing of her nipples slowly morphed into pleasure, his smacks grew harder, eliciting a moan from her even as she lifted and shoved back for more.

Jack chuckled at her eager response, loving the bright red hue covering her round cheeks and her now warm, stiff nipples that were poking his palm. A few more hard swats across both buttocks and then he moved behind her to run his fingers through her wet slit.

Morgan cried out when he thrust two fingers into her pussy, ruthlessly driving her to a fast and furious climax. It took every effort to remain bent over, in position, as he drove her to heights of ecstasy she had only ever achieved with him. Shaken, she barely heard him when he demanded, "Again," and could do nothing but obey as his skillful fingers worked her sheath with masterful strokes, bringing her to another swift orgasm.

She whimpered with the slow removal of his fingers from her still spasming pussy, then shuddered on a low moan when he drew them up to circle her anus before pushing with slow, relentless intention into her tight, forbidden hole.

"Jack!" she cried out at the pleasure/pain as he filled her, then whimpered at the sharp crack of his free hand on her thigh.

"What do you call me?"

"Master... please, it's too much." Morgan thought it would be weird calling the man she has known since she was a kid 'master,' but the ease with which the title escaped her mouth surprised her as did how right it sounded in this situation.

"Did you know some women can come from anal stimulation alone? I wonder if you're one of those women."

Morgan buried her head in her arms, her body covered

in a light sheen of perspiration, shaking from the onslaught of sensations. His fingers were huge in her ass, but the pain of their entry soon proved stimulating as he stroked sensitive nerve endings that sent pulsing heat down to her empty pussy. It took only moments before she pushed back against his shallow thrusts, accepting his invasion of her most private orifice and the pleasure he wrought from her. When Jack used his free hand to glide over her smooth lips, spreading her juices before slapping against her pussy, she screamed with her body's blistering, heated response.

Again and again, in tandem with his thrusting fingers, his hand smacked against her soft, damp flesh, wringing even more pleasure from her. Succumbing to the sensory overload, Morgan let go and came apart. Lifting her hips for more, spreading her legs wider for easier access, she relished each ruthless stroke into her ass and each sharp slap against her bare labia until she once again screamed out her pleasure.

Jack gave her no chance to catch her breath or her thoughts before shoving down his jeans and driving into her reddened, hot pussy. Her slick walls clasped around his cock and held him in a tight fist as he pummeled her depths with deep, hard strokes. He didn't expect her to come again, and thus was astonished when she gripped him with another orgasm, her climax gushing over his cock in damp relief, her walls milking his own come from him. Grasping her hips, he took her hard and fast, holding her still in a tight grip for his invasion and to ensure she didn't collapse on him. The pleasure of fucking her swamped his senses, damn near driving him to his knees.

Jack slowly pulled from her clinging warmth and lifted her off the counter, turning her into his arms. "Are you all right?" When she giggled and snuggled into him, he had his answer.

"I've got to quit challenging you. I won't survive if I don't."

"Good advice, but I doubt if you heed it for long. Why

don't you go soak in the bath for an hour while I start dinner?"

· · · · · · ·

Morgan winced as she sank down into the deep tub filled with swirling hot water. She hadn't realized how sore she was until now, but the blessed warmth and pulsating jets went a long way toward easing her discomfort. Laying her head back on the cushioned headrest, she sighed as her body relaxed and her mind wandered. She could get used to this. Just being around Jack was an aphrodisiac for her and recalling the feel of his hard cock moving with forceful strokes inside of her, stretching and filling her, was enough to cause her pussy to spasm with renewed need. *I'm insatiable*, she thought as she reached beneath the water to cup her pussy, the smooth folds soft and pliant beneath her fingers.

Jack leaned against the door, smiling. This was becoming a habit, he realized, spying on her as she pleasured herself. But not a habit he was anxious to break. Marc joined him just in time to see Morgan wince in discomfort.

"You might want to ease up a little," Marc admonished, frowning at Jack.

Morgan's eyes flew open at the sound of Marc's voice. Her hands went instinctively to cover herself as she glared at the two grinning men. "Do you mind?" she snapped, irritated at having her solitude interrupted.

"Actually, no, we don't." Jack smiled, ignoring her frown and glare. "Need help washing?"

"No, now get out, both of you."

"She's no fun," Marc complained, unruffled by her demand.

Raising a dark brow, Jack drawled, "I beg to differ, but we'll leave proof of that for this evening. Finish up, Morgan. I'm ready to put the steaks on."

The thought of food had her scrambling to obey. "Shoo.

I'll be out in a minute."

* * * * * * *

"You're really not considering taking her again tonight, are you?" Marc demanded as they walked back into the kitchen.

"Relax, papa bear," Jack returned dryly, checking the indoor grill for readiness. "I thought we'd scene with her together tonight, introduce her slowly to play in the club room, and give you a chance to get to know her better. You game?"

Marc turned from grabbing the plates. "Sure, as long as there's another available sub willing to let me finish with her."

"Like that's ever been a problem for you. There're several people in this group who are willing to share, as you well know."

"Are you sure you want to do this, Jack?"

Jack saw the pain in Marc's green eyes and heard the remorse in his voice. "She was too young and too inexperienced, Marc. Morgan isn't Cassie."

"She's older, but just as inexperienced. Doesn't that worry you?"

"You're the one who pushed me to go for it," Jack reminded him while tossing the steaks on the grill.

"But I didn't think you'd move so fast. What's the hurry?" Marc finished setting the table and retrieved a bottle of wine from a small wine refrigerator.

"Honestly, I'm not sure. I guess after waiting so long for her, I feel the need to tie her to me. We're both experienced enough to know if she's not receptive and neither of us will have a problem backing off."

"True. Okay, then let's put all our considerable skills and charm to work tonight so she'll never want to leave."

Jack had never allowed himself to even think about a future with Morgan that involved anything more than friendship, but in less than twenty-four hours he was hoping for just that. He couldn't recall any other woman who had responded with such open enthusiasm to his demands. The powerful combination of her natural acceptance coupled with her lush body would drive any dominate man insane with lust. But that look in her expressive whiskey eyes, the one that said she saw only him when she submitted, when she came, was what did it for him. To lose her now, after seeing that look and feeling her wet heat clasped around him, would kill him. Was it any wonder he had fought this so hard for so long?

Morgan padded into the kitchen wearing another one of his shirts, her hair damp and her face pink from her bath. Watching her hop onto a stool at the counter and cross her legs, he recalled how her soft thighs felt wrapped around him. "Hungry, princess?"

"Starving." Morgan smiled at him as he set a plate in front of her with a thick filet, baked potato, and salad.

"Me too." Marc took a seat on her right. "I'll take what you don't finish."

"Don't count on it, Marc," Jack said as he sat at her left. "My girl has always had a hearty appetite."

"Good to hear. Can't stand skinny scrawny women who eat nothing but rabbit food." Winking at her, Marc dug into his steak.

Morgan appreciated the compliments, appreciated even more knowing they were given to make her more comfortable with her body. Digging into her dinner, she listened as the two of them discussed the lodge and cabins. It soon became apparent their little getaway here was quite profitable and kept them busy year round.

"So, you rent to anyone, not just, uh... these special groups?" she asked, not sure what to call the people who were currently here for the weekend.

Jack smiled at her discomfort. "Yes, we rent to anyone. About half of our clientele come for BDSM play, some are swingers, some just couples who want to add a little exhibitionism to spice things up. We reserve certain blocks of time for the alternative lifestyle groups; the rest are families, college kids, or young couples vacationing."

"I'm assuming you change the club room for them?" She could just imagine the shock a young family would get if they walked into the club as it was set up now.

"Yes, and the cabins, which we'll equip for each renter per their requests. We have a large storage room where we stash the equipment when we're not using it."

Morgan ate her last bite of steak, savoring the tender meat grilled to perfection. Jack had remembered she liked her steak cooked medium rare, with a little pink. "That was wonderful, Jack. Thank you. Where do your guests go for meals?"

"Each cabin has a kitchen, utensils, dishes, and pans. Guests usually bring a supply of food, shop after they get here, or eat in one of the diners in Bear Creek, which is about twenty miles south of here and the closest town. We'll take you there this week. I imagine you didn't get to see much of it when you came through. You'll enjoy the little tourist shops and there's a bakery Marc can't seem to stay out of."

"Hey, can I help it if I have a sweet tooth? Find me a woman who can bake as well as Martha and I'll marry her in a heartbeat."

Morgan laughed when Marc gave her a hopeful look. "Forget it. I can't even boil water without causing a total disaster."

"That's no exaggeration, Marc, so be sure to keep her out of our kitchen. Except," Jack added with a smirk, "for when it comes time for dishes. Cleanup is your job." Leaning over, he kissed her nose before rising. "I'll be back up to get you shortly. Marc and I have to see to a few things downstairs for tonight's gathering. Don't bother changing, you look great just as you are."

"I am not going to parade around in front of all those people in nothing but your shirt again," Morgan stated with belligerence, forgetting his rules as she remembered the embarrassment of having her big butt bared in front of a room full of strangers.

Jack glanced at Marc and then nodded. Before Morgan realized what he intended, Marc had her bent over her stool and the shirt flipped up, baring her naked ass again. "Hey!" she squealed when he landed three hard smacks on her buttocks in rapid succession.

Jack grabbed her shoulders as she stood and glared at both men. "What do you say, Morgan?"

"Fine," she grumbled, mortified. "I'll wear the shirt."

"She's going to be a fun one, Jack," Marc said as the two of them walked out.

"I don't know which will be sorer, our hands or her ass," Jack replied.

Morgan cleaned up the kitchen with a silly grin on her face and tingling buttocks. She wasn't sure what Jack had planned for this evening, but she wouldn't give him any reason to give her another public spanking. Well, she didn't plan on it anyway. From the little she had witnessed of Jack's activities downstairs, she knew public play and bondage were a big part of the alternative lifestyle he'd been reluctant to share with her. If she had any hope of making this time with him last, she knew she'd have to submit to his wishes in places other than the privacy of his loft. She couldn't imagine having her well-endowed body naked and on display and not dying of sheer mortification, but she also could never have imagined her off-the-charts response to getting spanked in front of others.

Putting the last of the dishes away, she swore she'd do her best not to displease or embarrass Jack in front of his friends, even if it meant suffering the humiliation of letting others see her less than perfect body. She just had to remind herself Jack liked her the way she was, and that was all that mattered.

CHAPTER SIX

Jack held Morgan's hand as he led her into the club an hour later. Clad in nothing but his shirt, she felt conspicuous until she saw what some of the other women were wearing, or not wearing. The night before she had only a limited view of the large room from her hiding place and only a short time to take in the guests and activities before she was found out. At a seating area, she saw a naked woman kneeling between a man's knees, her mouth busy sucking his cock while he kept one hand fisted in her hair and casually sipped his drink with the other.

"Bill, are you and your pretty sub having a good time this weekend?" Jack asked, pulling her close to his side.

"We always do, Jack. I've had a hectic schedule the past few months and needed some down time. Who do we have here?" Bill nodded toward Morgan.

"This is Morgan. Morgan, Master Bill and Lori come up a few times a year. Bill's a district attorney and Lori's a teacher."

Morgan smiled and nodded at the couple, not sure what to say since Lori had her mouth filled with Bill's cock and made no move to release him to acknowledge the introduction. The two men discussed the excellent conditions for skiing for a few moments before they moved on.

"People sure aren't shy here, are they?" Morgan asked when they stopped in front of a scene area with a raised padded bench over which lay yet another naked woman.

"No, but everyone here has been in the lifestyle for a while. That's one of the reasons they come up here. They can get a nice ski trip and indulge in their alternate proclivities. There aren't too many places where people who enjoy bondage and domination can go to socialize, making it a lonely lifestyle at times. Watch. I think you'd enjoy this apparatus." Jack kept a close eye on Morgan's reaction, looking for signs of unease he might need to address before he went ahead with the scene he had planned for her.

The lowered head of the bench put the woman's ass on prominent display. An older, good-looking man moved behind her holding a round leather paddle, which he brought down with a resounding whack on her right buttock. Morgan shifted in unease as she watched the woman get a sound paddling, her ass turning bright red. Her pussy, clearly visible between her widely spread knees, revealed the damp proof of her excitement. She gasped or cried out with each strike of the paddle but her hips lifted in eager anticipation of the next one.

Morgan had no trouble recalling how the pain from her spanking this morning had turned to pleasure and how knowing Marc was watching added to her excitement. When Jack lowered his arm from around her waist and slid his big hand under the shirt so he could rub her buttocks, it took supreme willpower to bite back a moan of pleasure. *Maybe letting him pleasure me in public won't be as difficult as I'd imagined*, she thought as she leaned into his caresses.

Chuckling, Jack murmured in her ear, "I think you're ready for your own scene." He made one light graze over her slit before he grabbed her hand. "Come with me." He pulled her over to the dangling chain where he had tethered Sandy the night before. "Don't move," he instructed before striding to the back wall where various paddles and floggers and an assortment of cuffs hung.

Wary, Morgan watched him grab a set of cuffs, a flogger, and a long metal bar with cuffs attached on each end before returning to stand in front of her. When his hands went to the buttons on her shirt, Morgan couldn't keep from taking a quick, frantic look around to see who watched. "Jack, I mean master," she quickly amended when he scowled. "Wait."

"No, princess. If I wait, it'll give you too much time to think and right now I want you to feel." Spreading her shirt, he slipped a finger between her folds, watching as her eyes widened in first surprise then arousal. Removing his finger, he held up the glistening digit. "Watching Mindy get paddled excited you, as I knew it would. Trust me to know what you'll like. Can you do that?"

Morgan nodded her head before she lost her nerve. Jack slipped the shirt off then buckled the cuffs on her wrists, checking for tightness before raising her arms above her head and attaching the cuffs to the dangling chain. A heated blush started at her chest and crept up her neck to cover her face. Looking away from the people mingling nearby didn't ease her shame.

"Morgan, look at me," he demanded, moving in front of her so his big body blocked her view of the people moving past. "Keep your eyes on me and you'll be fine." Reaching out, he cupped a full breast and ran his thumb over the distended tip. "I think you're beautiful, and my opinion is all you need to concern yourself with. For tonight, all you have to say is stop if I do something you don't like or are uncomfortable with. Okay?"

"Okay, stop."

Grinning, he tweaked her nipple. "I'll ignore that." Kneeling, he attached the spreader bar to her ankles, leaving her open and vulnerable. Nodding to Marc, he moved to the wall, raised the chain until her arms were stretched tautly, watching her the whole time for signs of discomfort or stress. She was a little nervous, and a lot embarrassed, but otherwise kept her eyes on his and remained calm. "That's my girl," he praised her before picking up the flogger and moving behind her as Marc stepped in front of her. Perfect.

"Relax, darlin'," Marc said, his eyes calm and steady on hers when she pulled on the chain and her breath hitched in panic. "We're just going to make you feel good."

"We?" she squeaked, ignoring the way her heartbeat sped up with excitement. Morgan couldn't deny how her arousal spiked when she tested her bonds and discovered she had very little movement, or choice in what they had planned. Jack's praise and both men's calm, take-charge attitude went a long way in lessening the mortification of being bound naked in front of others and heightening her expectation.

"We," Jack whispered in her ear from behind her. Grabbing her hair, he turned her head and kissed her, hard. "Trust me."

Morgan looked up into his dark eyes a moment before nodding once.

"Good girl."

She basked in the additional praise that warmed her as much as his hot look. When Marc cupped her face, tilted her up until her lips met his, she sank against him, trusting both Jack and his friend to take care of her. Marc's lips were soft, coaxing her to open for his tongue. Just as she relaxed enough to enjoy his kiss and his lean body against hers, a snap of leather fell across her buttocks followed by a light sting that faded too soon. Marc pulled his mouth from hers, but she didn't have time to mourn the loss as he cupped her breasts, his fingers grasping her nipples as the flogger kissed her buttocks again.

Morgan embraced the dual assault on her senses, the light strokes of the flogger that left behind a biting sting that quickly warmed to pleasure, and the hard pinching of Marc's fingers on her nipples. It wasn't long before she was swaying back to meet the downward stroke of the flogger while thrusting her breasts into Marc's hands. Being restrained, unable to move her arms or legs, heightened her vulnerability and increased her pleasure, sensations she could get used to.

"You have lovely breasts, Morgan," Marc whispered before taking one taut peak into his mouth and pulling on it, his mouth sucking hard while he pulled and twisted her other nipple.

"Oh, God!" she gasped when Jack applied the flogger a little harder just as Marc pinched one nipple harder and took a deeper pull on the other one. Her buttocks burned, the burn turning to blistering heat that spread down to her pussy. Spasming in desperate need, she begged without shame, "Please, sir. Master Jack, please."

Both men chuckled at her stammered pleading but didn't relent in their torture. "Do you like the flogger, princess?" Jack asked right before landing a sharp strike across the top of her thighs.

"Yes," she yelped as the leather bit against her tender thighs and then again across her ass. When Marc moved a hand down her waist and caressed her bare pussy lips, she couldn't keep from thrusting against him, begging for a deeper touch.

"Such soft lips," Marc murmured, stroking her labia before spreading her folds and slipping two fingers into her slick sheath. "Mmmm, soft in here too, and wet. Very, very wet." His lips came down on hers again, harder this time as his fingers went deeper.

When Marc's thumb rasped against her clit the same time as the flogger landed with a wicked snap across both buttocks, she screamed out her pleasure. The climax erupted with unforgiving speed and force, leaving her gasping and shaking.

Jack dropped the flogger and ran his hand over Morgan's striped, red buttocks and thighs before delving between her legs and slipping into her still spasming vagina. When she leaned back against him in total trust, he smiled at Marc around her damp body. "Again, Morgan."

Morgan moaned, shaking her head. "I can't."

"Sure you can. Here, we'll show you."

And then Jack finger-fucked her from behind, his hands slipping between her legs and her buttocks to delve deeply into both orifices. With Marc's lips back on her nipples and his fingers joining Jack's between her legs, they both brought her to another quick, stunning peak that rivaled the first one for intensity.

Exhausted and sated from sensory overload, her mind still in an orgasm-induced fog, she never noticed when the men released her and Jack carried her to a chair, cuddling her on his lap. She barely remembered drinking a bottle of water he practically poured down her throat before being carried upstairs and tucked into bed.

Morgan fell asleep alone, but woke when Jack joined her several hours later. Feeling him pull her next to his hard body, she had no trouble falling back asleep.

• • • • • • •

Being careful, Jack picked up Morgan's left hand, raised it above her head, and attached the wrist cuff, pleased she had not woken yet. She had climaxed so beautifully last night while restrained, he wanted to see her do it again and again. Damn if she hadn't surpassed all his hopes already, not only enjoying his sexual preferences, but embracing them with wholehearted enthusiasm despite her obvious discomfort with her naked body. Her soft moan when she shifted as he cuffed her right wrist had his cock stirring. Since he'd refrained from taking her again last night, he was more than ready to feel her tight sheath clasping his cock again. But first, he needed to finish binding her. Gently lifting her left leg, he wrapped a larger cuff around her thigh and tightened the strap, leaving her leg bent and pulled to the side. After doing the same with her right leg, he sat back and viewed his handiwork. Knees bent and spread, hips lifted, she lay open and ready for his use.

Running his hands over her legs, he bent down and took a slow lick up her seam, eliciting another soft moan from her. "Wake up, princess. It's time to play." Using his thumbs, he pulled her smooth folds further apart, revealing the pink, wet walls of her pussy. "You're so pretty, Morgan, pretty enough to eat." Another deep stroke of his tongue had her eyes flying open and her hips jerking against his mouth. Chuckling, he murmured, "There you are," before diving back in to feast on her succulent flesh.

Morgan woke to the torturous sensations of Jack's mouth between her legs, his beard rasping against her tender skin, and instinctively tried to lower her arms to grasp him anywhere she could. When she couldn't budge, her arousal spiked even higher, her hips jerking against his face. Who would have thought being rendered immobile during sex could be so exciting? When his fingers joined his tongue in her pussy, she strained harder toward his mouth, whimpering in frustration and unfulfilled need. "Jack, master, please."

Jack looked up at her lush breasts as they jiggled with her failed efforts then at her flushed face. "I like hearing you beg almost as much as I like hearing you come. Come for me now, Morgan."

"Oh, God."

He gave her no time to take a breath before delving inside her again, getting down to using his tongue, teeth, and fingers to bring her to a shattering climax. The strong suction of his lips on her clit had her shaking, the small bite of his teeth had her screaming, and the deep strokes of his fingers had her coming apart over and over until she couldn't tell when one orgasm stopped and another began.

Moving up her slick body, he stopped to suckle her hard little nipples before taking her mouth in a deep kiss. Morgan tasted herself on his tongue as she kissed him back with greedy fervor, forgetting to breathe as their lips dueled for possession. Moaning into his mouth, she licked every essence of herself from his tongue before doing the same with his lips, loving the feel of his whiskers against her cheeks.

"You've got a very talented tongue, princess. Why don't you show me what else you can do with it?"

Smiling, she replied, "I'd love to," before opening her mouth to reciprocate the pleasure he had given her.

Jack straddled her face, grabbed the headboard between her restrained arms, and dipped his cock into her mouth, cursing as her lips wrapped around him and her tongue explored every inch of his dick. Careful not to go too deep, he took shallow dips in and out of her mouth, the strong suction of her cheeks and coaxing swirls of her tongue around his girth coming close to making him come right then. "Fuck, you're good at this. I'd be jealous if I wasn't enjoying your obvious experience so much."

Morgan could have told him she had very little experience in giving head simply because she had never cared for the act before now. But, as with everything else he had done with and to her, she discovered there was little she couldn't imagine enjoying with Jack. His cock was big, both in length and width, and filled her mouth almost to the point of discomfort. She liked learning the taste and the feel of every hard ridge. When he pulled up again, she tightened her clasped lips around the plum-shaped head and sucked it like a lollipop, drawing another curse from Jack. Pre-come coated her tongue, and she lapped it up, disappointed when he pulled away from her before she got the chance to taste all of him in her mouth.

"But you didn't…" she complained when he scooted down and settled between her spread knees.

"Next time," he replied, his voice gruff as he shoved his cock into her pussy. "Right now I need to fuck you."

"Oh, okay," she gasped, accepting his forceful, deep thrusts inside her with eager lifts of her hips, the leather straps biting into her thighs adding to the onslaught of sensations spiraling out of control.

"Shit, I'm not going to last. You feel too fucking good. Come with me," he demanded, reaching down to press her clit even harder against his pummeling cock, making her cry out as she soaked his cock with her come. "Yes." Taking her mouth with as much ruthless intent as he took her body, he pounded into her, his cock filling her womb with his seed.

When he reached up to release her arms, Morgan clasped them around his sweat-slick back, loving the feel of his large hard body moving against hers as his strokes slowed and they both caught their breath. "I could quickly become a morning person if I got to wake up like that all the time," she whispered in his ear.

"Neither one of us would survive if we greeted each morning like this. But, what the hell, let's give it a try." Laughing, Jack pulled away from her before he gave in to temptation and took her again. Releasing her legs, he pulled her from the bed. "Up you go. I need to be on time to take our guests to the slopes this morning. Get going." Giving her a hard swat on the ass, he pushed her toward the bathroom.

Rubbing her abused cheek, she glared at him. "You go ahead. I want to work on my sketches this morning. I'll see you when you get back."

Smiling at the bright red hand print on her butt, he itched to add a matching one to her other cheek, but held back. "All right, but if you go out, stay around the lodge. It's easy to get turned around out here and lose your way."

"One trek through those trees in knee-deep snow was enough for me. I'm not going anywhere."

• • • • • • •

Sitting in front of the windows with a cup of tea an hour later, the abrupt ringing of her cell phone interrupted her peaceful solitude. "Hello, mother," she answered in resignation, bracing herself for another lecture.

"Morgan, I just found out you're with Jack Sinclair, that roughneck boy who used to work for us," Kathleen greeted her in a snide tone.

"He's not nor has he ever been a roughneck, mother," Morgan sighed. "He worked very hard for you and daddy and did a beautiful job keeping your property looking nice." And an even better job befriending your lonely neglected little girl, she was tempted to say.

"I knew I should've put a stop to you hanging around him so much. Really, Morgan, you can't seriously think of giving up a catch like Joel for a man like him. I won't hear of it. Why, your father and I would never be able to live the scandal down. I insist you come home immediately. Your engagement party is still scheduled for next Saturday."

"Dammit, mother," Morgan burst out, letting her anger surface. "I told you before I left to cancel it, that the wedding is off. How can you want me to marry him after what he did?" She didn't love Joel, but his betrayal still hurt.

"Don't curse at me, young lady. And really, what did he do that was so awful? Women can't really expect a man not to stray once in a while, dear, especially someone like you who doesn't have many prospects to begin with. If you had taken after me and been blessed with a petite body or at least been passably attractive, you could be a little choosier. As it is, I've smoothed things over for you and Joel is willing to take you back. I'll tell your father to expect you back at work this week," she stated firmly, confident her wishes would be met.

Ignoring the seeds of doubt her mother planted, she firmed her voice. "Again, I'm not coming home right now, and when or if I do, it won't be to pick up where I left off. There will be no wedding, at least not to Joel."

"Don't tell me that man has asked you to marry him!"

Her mother's appalled voice would have made her laugh if Morgan wasn't so upset over the disbelief in her tone. The truth was, Jack hadn't said a word about her staying with him and she wondered if he expected her to leave after a few days, and wanted their relationship to return to friends only after the weather cleared enough for her to get home. The thought of returning home to her boring, unsatisfying job and lonely apartment was depressing and something she didn't want to think about.

"No," she sighed, "he hasn't asked me to marry him, so you can quit panicking. I don't know how long I'm going to stay here, but in the meantime, I suggest you cancel any and all wedding plans and tell Joel I meant it when I told him to go to hell. Goodbye, mother."

As always, speaking with her mother left Morgan emotionally drained and insecure, and more so since they'd argued. She wished she knew how Jack felt about their new relationship. He seemed happy now to have her here, and she knew she pleased him sexually, but as far as anything permanent between them, that had never come up. One thing was for certain. Even if she didn't stay here with Jack like she wanted to, she wouldn't return to her old life. Somehow, she'd find a way to pursue her art and make a living at it, and it wouldn't be in Chicago or anywhere near her parents. Looking out at the snow-covered landscape, right now somewhere down south sounded pretty good.

After heating up leftovers she found in the fridge for lunch, Morgan decided she needed some exercise and since there was so much snow, the only thing she could think of was building a snowman. After dressing in a pair of jeans and sweater, she tugged knee-high snow boots on over her pants, zipped up her heavy jacket, and pulled on mittens before trudging outside. With everyone either on the slopes or in town checking out the shops and restaurants, eerie quietness greeted her as she stepped out into the bright glare bouncing off the snow-covered ground.

Trying not to think about her mother's phone call, Morgan had fun working on a snowman. Used to entertaining herself ever since she was a child, especially when Jack wasn't around, she had no problem killing time until he returned. By the time he came driving up, she had completed a four-foot figure and beamed proudly at it as Jack got out of the Tahoe.

Jack grinned at the large mounds on the chest. "Let me guess," he called out to her, "a snow woman, right?"

"Of course. Come on, Jack. Let's build one together."

Jack was tempted, especially since she looked awfully cute with her hood up and tied snugly under her chin, the fur trim framing her pink face. But he was cold and tired and needed a break before the get-together tonight, which would be the last one before this group checked out tomorrow. "Later, princess. I'm going to warm up."

After he turned to head inside, she pissed him off with a well-aimed snowball smacking the back of his head. Shaking the snow out of his hair, he glared at her. "Morgan, stop it right…" Before he could finish, another snowball landed against his chest.

Laughing at his incredulous look, Morgan pleaded, "Come on, Jack. Just for a little bit. I haven't had anyone to play with all afternoon."

Jack couldn't keep from succumbing to her cajoling and enthusiasm for the simple play. He couldn't count how many times she had used that line on him growing up. Shoving aside his tiredness, he warned, "You're going to be sorry." Scooping up snow as he trudged toward her, he pelted her with snowballs faster than she could retaliate.

Squealing, Morgan tried to return some shots of her own, but it soon became obvious Jack had a lot more practice at snowball fights than she had. Her only recourse was to run, but she soon discovered he also had more practice running in deep snow. Within seconds, he had her tackled and hauled against him, their cold lips fusing together.

"It was very bad of you not to listen to me, princess. Plus, you lost," Jack said against her mouth, their cold breath mingling.

Out of breath from laughing and running, Morgan panted, "You cheated."

"How so?"

"I don't know, I just know you did."

"Mmm, seems to me you've used that line on me also over the years, usually when you lost at whatever we were playing."

"And then you'd let me win." She gave him her best hopeful little girl look.

"Not gonna happen this time. This time, you'll suffer grownup consequences for defying me." Grabbing her hand, he pulled her over to a gazebo with benches built onto the sides.

Sputtering, Morgan asked, "What are you doing? Let's go in, I'm cold."

Jack undid her jeans with quick, deft fingers, shoved them down, and pulled her over his lap as he sat down. "One guess as to what I'm doing."

"Damn it, Jack, it's freezing out here!" she complained, all humor having fled when she realized his intentions. "Let me up! What if someone sees?"

Chuckling, Jack landed a hard swat on her ass. "Wouldn't be the first time. Don't worry, I'll give you a quick warm-up."

She was cold and embarrassed, more so when she saw Marc pull up and he and two couples took their time unloading their skis while Jack peppered her wriggling ass with swift, hard slaps. But as usual, it took only moments for the pain encompassing her buttocks to turn her on. Cursing, she turned her head away from her grinning audience and quit struggling. True to his word, his ass did warm quickly under his hand until her cold buttocks burned, each smack a little harder, each response a little more needy. Her mortification knew no bounds as she pictured herself all bundled up against the cold with only her white buttocks naked and on display. Having her butt bare left her more vulnerable and exposed than if he had stripped her naked. At least then, she wouldn't know what part of her body people were staring at. Imagining what her ass looked like added to her embarrassment, but the heat and pain from Jack's unrelenting, hard hand aroused her nonetheless.

"Jack, please, please make me come," she sobbed, ashamed of her desperation.

"Poor baby," Jack crooned, running his hand over her warm, red cheeks. "You do feel a little warm here. But, since you're being punished, it wouldn't be prudent of me to reward you with an orgasm, now would it?" Even as he said that, he ran his fingers in a light caress over her dripping slit before entering her just far enough to feel the tight clasp of her slick walls.

"But," she protested, twisting to glare up at him, "you enjoyed our snowball fight, and you won!"

"Still, I was tired and cold and didn't want to play right then. But you ignored my warning to stop. Now that I've warmed you up, I think I'll cool you off again."

Remembering the ice on her nipples, Morgan cringed as she saw Jack reach behind him, just outside the gazebo, and scoop up snow. "No, Jack!" she cried out while trying to roll off his lap, but he was too fast and too strong for her.

Relishing his immense enjoyment at her expense, Jack grabbed her around the waist, held her down, and rubbed snow onto her red, squirming buttocks, her curses ringing in his ears. A few more hard swats on her snow-covered ass increased her struggles and complaints but several more and his threat to continue until she stopped had her lying in a docile heap over his lap. Taking pity on her shivering form, he let her up, pulled her jeans over her wet, sore ass, and grinned up into her scowling face. "All done, princess."

"Don't you 'princess' me, you big jerk. My ass is sore and freezing and you owe me an orgasm." Turning, she stomped into the lodge, ignoring all of them.

"She's got a temper," Marc said as he walked with Jack back into the lodge. "And a nice ass."

"Yes, she does." Jack's little tussle had invigorated him and made him hard. Then again, Morgan didn't have to do much to get an erection out of him.

"Do you have plans for her tonight?"

"Yeah, I've got something in mind. Want to help?" When Marc hesitated, Jack asked, "What's wrong?"

"I just don't want to see you make the same mistake I did. If this is serious between you two, how far do you want the sharing to go?"

"Shit, sorry, Marc. I wasn't thinking." Jack had been there the night Marc had planned to share Cassie with him, and he had been there in the days following, supporting his friend through the anguish of knowing he had pushed her too hard too fast. Cassie had been too young and naïve to see Marc's actions weren't because he didn't care, but because he cared so much he wanted to give her the ultimate pleasure of having two men. "Morgan's not Cassie and we have a lengthy history behind us, as you've repeatedly mentioned. She knows how much I care, and that there's nothing I won't do for her. To answer your question, I intended to just torture her some more today with your help until I have her on the cross tonight. I figure between the two of us, we can have her so frustrated and ready for an orgasm, she won't think twice about me taking her in public."

"I think I can help you with that." Smiling, they entered the lodge in search of their prey.

CHAPTER SEVEN

Thinking there had to be something perversely wrong with her to get turned on by such humiliating, uncomfortable treatment, Morgan stripped out of her damp clothes. The shock of cold snow on top of heated smacks numbed her buttocks and her mind until irritation broke through. Then to leave her hanging only added insult to injury. Their amusement at her expense had her cursing both men as she dried off, rubbing the towel up and down her chilled body with brisk, jerky movements. She was still swearing when Jack strolled into the bedroom. "I did not enjoy that, Jack," she snapped, irritated to see a lack of remorse while she stood there freezing.

"Poor baby," he crooned. "Here, let me help get you warm."

Sidestepping his outstretched hand, she grumbled, "I don't need your help."

"Morgan."

Damn it. Why did that warning tone have to replace the lingering chill in her body with heated awareness? Yes, it was definite there was something wrong with her. "My butt hurts."

Her petulant reply made Jack smile. Snatching the towel

from her, he rubbed the nubby cloth over her breasts, adding pressure in a circular motion over her nipples before moving down her waist. Kneeling, he draped the towel over his palm and ran it up between her legs, his grin widening when she parted them without instruction.

Bracing her hands on his big shoulders as he rubbed between her legs, she was unable to stifle a moan when his ministrations added to her frustrating, unfulfilled desire. She warmed inside and out, his hot breath on her thigh adding to her arousal in a way she didn't need. In an unconscious gesture, she thrust her pelvis forward, a silent plea for more she had no control over.

Chuckling, Jack rose, drew his arms around her as he switched the towel to her ass, and rubbed her buttocks as his mouth took hers in a demanding, wet kiss. When she melted against him, her pelvis grinding against the rigid length of his cock, he pulled away, draped the towel over her shoulders, and quipped, "There. I think you're all warmed up now. Slip on my shirt and come help me with dinner." The damp towel hit him in the back as he made a speedy exit, her curses following him out of the room.

Morgan was tempted to lock herself in the bathroom and relieve her frustration herself, but the mention of food reminded her of her other unfulfilled hunger. She obeyed Jack by slipping his shirt on, but added a dry pair of jeans under it, knowing it would piss him off.

"What're we having?" she asked, strolling into the kitchen barefoot.

Jack looked up from chopping potatoes and tossing them into a large pot. He frowned, noticing her jeans, then laid his knife down and moved toward her with slow, measured steps.

Morgan backed away from him, not trusting the gleam in his eyes. Backing into a hard body put an abrupt halt to her retreat and Marc's arms circling her from behind made sure she stayed in place.

"Now what has she done?" Marc asked before he ran his

lips up the side of her neck.

"She put on jeans when I specifically told her to put on my shirt." Jack stopped in front of her, smiling at her look of defiance. Something had happened while he was out earlier to make Morgan act out, and if he were to guess, he bet she'd received another call from one of her parents. She was always at her brattiest or her quietest after a confrontation with her mother or father. "Take off the jeans, Morgan," he ordered, his soft, warning tone giving her no quarter.

"I'm still cold and I only have to bow down to your will when it comes to sex, and since we're not having sex, I'll wear what I want." *But hopefully we'll have sex soon*, she thought, Marc's lean hard body bracing her adding fuel to a fire already blazing hot.

"I think she needs some help, Jack." Marc kept his left arm tight around her waist as he unsnapped her jeans.

Morgan's breath hitched with excitement as Jack shoved them down, but she refused to make it easy for them. Kicking out, she fought to keep Jack from pulling them completely off. Her struggles caused her shirt to bunch up, revealing the bare lips of her shaved pussy. Marc used his free hand to cup between her legs, his palm covering her mound, holding her in a tight clasp. Biting her lip in frustration, Morgan held back a moan as Jack stripped the jeans from her.

"Marc, my sub needs to be punished for disobeying me, but I think her ass is too sore for another spanking right now," Jack said.

"Well, there's only one other thing to do then," Marc agreed, right before his hand pulled away from her pussy to slap against her sensitive folds with a jarring smack.

The startling pain elicited a cry from her, his hand landing in a barrage of steady slaps again and again. The short, rapid succession of stinging swats heated her tender folds, her whimpers going unheeded as Jack watched Marc mete out her punishment. Within moments, her perverse acceptance of their treatment had her enjoying the warm throbbing between her legs. With her juices creaming her thighs, she couldn't keep from thrusting against his descending palm, meeting and welcoming each painful slap.

Biting her lip, she locked her eyes on Jack's, imploring, "Please, master, please."

"Stop."

Marc stopped, his hand damp from her juices. Looking down into Morgan's red face, he saw what Jack had seen. Morgan was on the verge of climax and a few more well-aimed slaps would have sent her flying. "Poor darling." Rubbing his fingers over the soft flesh he had just tormented, he continued to stimulate her to the edge of orgasm before backing off.

Tears filled her eyes as Marc caressed her sensitive folds then dipped between them to stroke over her inflamed clit, only to retreat before she could come. All the while, Jack stood in front of her, arms crossed, watching out of those dark, enigmatic eyes. "Damn it, you two, quit teasing me. I can't take it anymore," she cried out when Marc once again teased her clit just to deny her the relief she was in desperate need of.

Jack kissed her on the nose and nodded at Marc. "Come help me get this stew going, or we'll never eat."

Marc released her and joined Jack at the counter where the two of them resumed cutting vegetables as if nothing happened. And, damn it, nothing *had* happened as far as she was concerned. She knew Jack well enough to know he didn't do anything without an ulterior motive; she just had to figure out what that motive was, because right now she didn't have a clue. Striving for nonchalance as if she hadn't been begging only moments before, Morgan joined them in preparing the beef stew. Within minutes, the three of them were laughing as Marc and Jack told her about some of the spills and antics the guests had pulled that afternoon.

Morgan's hopes that Jack had finished toying with her were dashed when he unbuttoned her shirt and flipped it open before boosting her onto a stool between him and Marc for dinner. Even though she had gotten comfortable being naked in front of Jack, she still felt self-conscious in front of Marc, more so with both of them being fully dressed. His green eyes lit with appreciation when he looked at her, but years of hearing her mother put her down for her larger figure left her with insecurities that were hard to suppress.

Grabbing the edges of the shirt, she pulled them closed, retorting, "I'm not sitting here exposed while we eat."

Attuned to her every nuance, Jack noticed her uncertain glance at Marc before she turned her glare up at him. "Yes," he stated implacably, "you are." Pulling the shirt from her tight-fisted grasp, he spread it open again. "You're so pretty, Morgan. Surely you don't want to deny us the pleasure of looking at you."

Marc, taking his cue from Jack, added, "Gorgeous. Soft in all the right places." Reaching over, he cupped a full breast, kneading the soft, pliant flesh. "It's no wonder Jack's had a hard-on for you for years. If it had been me, I sure as hell couldn't have refrained from taking you for so long."

Morgan's startled eyes flew from the sincerity reflected on his face to see Jack frown and mutter, "Shut up, Marc." Hearing he wanted her long before she arrived in Colorado gave her a warm fuzzy feeling to go along with the ripple of irritation his stubbornness in keeping her at arm's length always induced.

Marc was handsome, nice, and his hands knew their way around a woman's body. She didn't crave any man but Jack as a lover, but if he wanted to add to her pleasure by giving Marc certain liberties, who was she to argue? He was the master after all, she thought with an inward smile.

"Eat, princess, you'll need your strength for tonight." Jack intentionally relieved her from the awkwardness with his disconcerting statement. Throughout dinner, he and Marc conversed casually while every once in a while caressing Morgan's breasts, legs, or soft folds, keeping her arousal high and on edge. Their touches didn't affect her appetite, he noted, as she ate her whole bowl of stew even as her eyes grew glassy and her legs tightened together in an effort to ease her frustration. By the end of dinner, he was satisfied she was ready and so eager to be taken by him she wouldn't care where they were or who was watching.

An hour later, Morgan was so ready to get laid she could literally scream with the frustration, but when she realized Jack meant to take her downstairs in front of a room full of strangers, her insecurities dampened her excitement. She was just now getting comfortable bringing Marc into their scenes; the very idea of being taken in front of strangers wedged a lump of unease in her throat.

"You're awfully quiet," Jack commented, handing her a plate to dry. He had stayed to help her do the dishes while Marc went downstairs to greet their guests, her silence since he mentioned taking her downstairs speaking volumes.

"You've given me a lot to think about," she said, hoping he'd think she referred to their titillating touches throughout dinner.

"What's bothering you, Morgan? And don't give me some bullshit answer. This is me you're talking to. Am I moving too fast?"

"No!" Her swift denial gave away her fear he'd reject her if she didn't go along with him. She was unsure about fucking in public, but not about wanting to be with him for as long as he'll have her.

Pinning her against the counter with his arms braced behind her, he held her gaze with his. "Out with it."

"Fine," she snapped, irritation overriding insecurities. "I don't want you to fuck me in front of all those people. But I will if that's what you want."

"Sorry, princess. It doesn't work that way. I thought you trusted me?"

"I do." Her brows furrowed as she wondered why he thought she didn't.

"If you did, then you'd know I would never subject you

to anything I wasn't sure you'd enjoy. I would never put you in a position you weren't comfortable with. Well," he amended with a rueful grin, "a position you weren't mentally comfortable with."

Thinking of the uncomfortable hot then cold outdoor butt experience, Morgan returned his smile, relaxing. "This is important to you?"

"Yes, but not as important as your well-being. I don't want you to go home regretting anything that has happened between us. That's why I didn't want to start this in the first place," he reminded her.

He didn't know it, but he just settled the matter for her. If he wasn't planning on their affair continuing past the next day or two, she would damn well suck up her insecurities and get the most out of this time with Jack as she could. Ignoring the way her heart broke a little at his last remark, she smiled up at him. "Give me a few minutes and I'll be ready."

Little did she know two nights ago wearing nothing but Jack's shirt in his club would become a habit. After washing up, she hurried back into the great room before she changed her mind.

Morgan could now put a few names with faces and their friendly greetings eased the chill brought on by nerves. Crouching in hiding to watch the goings on was a far cry from participating, but she still found it exciting to watch others. Jack had explained how a lot of these people frequented strict BDSM clubs where certain protocol was demanded at all times as well as strict dress codes and modes of address. Here, there were no such rules, leaving such matters up to their guests to decide how they wanted to spend their vacation. The lodge provided a safe, fun getaway where they could indulge in their alternative lifestyle if they wished and to whatever extent they wished. As long as they obeyed the drinking limits and their play remained safe, sane, and consensual, they were free to do as they pleased.

Jack held Morgan's hand as he walked with her through

the club, socializing until she relaxed enough to set aside her insecurities. She wasn't shy about watching or asking questions about the different equipment. An hour later and after one strong rum and coke, her whiskey eyes rounded with lust as she watched a dom take his restrained sub on one of the raised padded benches, she was more than ready to indulge in a little play of their own.

"Come, princess. I believe I see a cross with your name on it."

Morgan's unease returned when Jack stopped in front of a large, padded wooden X set up in a well-lit scene area. Restraints were attached at the end of each post. When she took an instinctive step back, Jack tugged on her hand, drawing her wary gaze up to his.

"Trust me?" he asked, waiting patiently for her response.

Recalling the scene they had just witnessed and how the restrained woman had cried out in pleasure as soon as that man's hard cock penetrated her, had her curious about her own response to being taken while bound, but the thought of such a personal act performed in public still made her balk. "What are you going to do?"

"Whatever I want. Morgan," he said as he released her hand and cupped her face. "You know I'm not going to do anything you don't want." Sliding one hand slowly down her chest then up under her shirt, he caressed her damp sheath, never taking his eyes from hers. A few strokes of his fingers and she was thrusting against his hand; a brush of his thumb over her swollen, sensitive clit had her whimpering. Using his other hand, he quickly unbuttoned the shirt and slipped it off her shoulders. "Come, stand with your back to the cross and trust me to make you feel good."

Morgan ignored the warm flush creeping up from her neck and kept her face averted from the few people mingling close enough to watch them as she moved into position. Shielding her with his big body, Jack restrained her hands and feet in lined cuffs, leaving her spread open, bare and vulnerable. To her shame, her arousal spiked up another notch, just as it had last night when he had chained her to be pleasured by both him and Marc. Only last night, Jack had assured her they wouldn't go any further than they did, concentrating on nothing but bringing her pleasure. Tonight he wasn't giving her any such assurances.

"You're so pretty, Morgan," Jack reassured her, stepping back to look his fill. Restrained, spread for his use, her lush body drew him like a magnet. The more he took her, the more he thirsted for her, until nothing slaked his need except being inside her. His large hands cupped her soft breasts as he ordered, "Look at me, and only me. Nothing and no one else matters except the two of us."

Morgan had no trouble obeying his command. His hands felt wonderful kneading her breasts, and when his fingers clasped her nipples and pinched those tender buds, she couldn't stifle her moan nor keep from pushing into his hands.

Chuckling, Jack leaned down and took her mouth in a rough kiss, swallowing her gasp as he stroked her tongue in rhythm with his stroking thumbs over her nipples.

"Jack, master, please," she begged when he pulled his mouth from hers, all the earlier teasing returning to send her into quick arousal.

"Please what?"

"More."

"Well, that's easy enough to give you." Jack's lips replaced his fingers on her breasts, his mouth moving between first one nipple and then the other, his strong suction of each tender bud heightening her need. After both nipples were cherry red and hardened into stiff points, he reached into his pocket and retrieved a set of nipple clamps she hadn't known he'd brought with him.

"What are you doing?" Morgan asked, eyeing the small clamps with trepidation.

"Giving you more like you asked." At her squealed curse when he attached the first clamp, he adjusted the ring, loosening it a tad. "Take a deep breath. The pain will ease in a moment," he assured her.

Within seconds the pain subsided and her nipple throbbed with swollen numbness, an odd sensation that wasn't altogether unpleasant. When he moved to her other nipple, she sucked in a quick breath, prepared this time for that first snap of pain.

"There. Don't you look pretty?" Jack licked each nipple, relishing her soft whimper. When he delved between her spread thighs and met soaking wet flesh, he knew he couldn't wait any longer. Releasing his cock, he thrust into her, not giving her time to think, only to feel.

Morgan screamed as she came apart; her pussy so long denied clasped around his hard length and refused to let go as the tremors from her instant release raced through her body. Tossing her head back, she forgot about where they were, about her reticence over being fucked in public and succumbed to the pleasure sizzling through her veins. Over and over he pounded into her, Jack's hands clasping hers as he relentlessly brought her to peak after peak.

"Oh, God!" she cried out as she struggled to get closer to him, lifting her hips to meet each hard thrust, her thighs quivering as she strained to take him deeper. The room in front of her blurred into a kaleidoscope of colors, the faces of those watching them adding to the bright, explosive excitement. She now knew why he had toyed with her for so long upstairs without giving her relief.

Morgan's pussy rippling around him was too much for Jack to resist as were her soft, mewling cries of release and her glazed, pleasure-filled eyes. Letting go of her hands, he grabbed her buttocks and held her hips toward him as he thrust once, twice, three more times before exploding in a climax so powerful he saw stars.

Morgan looked down, dazed, watching as he held her hips so tight she couldn't move. His cock was red and wet as he slowed his thrusts, his come warm as it filled her. They were both perspiring and panting heavily when he pulled out of her, leaving her feeling bereft and empty. "Let's go upstairs," she whispered, wanting to continue their lovemaking in private.

Smiling, Jack kissed her nose and adjusted his clothing. "I think I've created a monster." Releasing her, he hugged her soft, sated body before slipping her shirt back on but leaving it unbuttoned. "Come on, princess. Let's get you some water." Accepting a bottle of water from Marc, Jack led Morgan to an empty sofa and sat down, pulling her onto his lap. After she'd downed most of the water, he held her shaking body, running his hand over her clamped nipples, down her soft waist, and over her bent legs before taking the same journey in reverse.

"You were beautiful up there, Morgan," he murmured as she relaxed and came down from the high such an intense experience usually caused. "I like how you don't hide from your passions."

"I was loud, wasn't I?" she whispered, her facing turning a delightful pink.

"Yes, you were, and I was the envy of every dom here."

Morgan smiled at his smug look, doubting his words, but relishing the intention behind them. Tucking her head into his shoulder, she relaxed against him, enjoying the soothing strokes of his hand. Her contentment was short-lived, however, when his hand stopped on her right breast and grasped the nipple clamp.

"Ready?" he asked, but before she could ask what for, he removed the clamp. With a yelp, she slapped her hand over her nipple as the blood flow resumed and sent sharp needles of pain through her whole breast.

Grasping her hand, Jack shoved it aside, took the poor abused bud into his mouth, and suckled. When she relaxed, he hastened to remove the other one and latch onto to it, licking away the pain as she wiggled and panted in discomfort. By the time he had eased the pain, her arousal had been reignited, as was his.

• • • • • • •

They couldn't keep this pace up, Morgan thought, stumbling into the shower the next morning, her sore body protesting every movement. She had been asleep a scant two hours after calling it a night around midnight when Jack had woken her with a sharp abrupt smack on her ass. Laughing at her screech of outrage, he'd pulled up her hips and thrust into her, stating she was the one who mentioned continuing what they started downstairs.

As usual, her body had responded to the demands of his and within moments she was pushing back against him, welcoming his invasion as his hard possession drove the breath from her body.

Leaning her head back, Morgan let the hot water cascade over her face and shoulders, the heat seeping into her aching muscles. She was looking forward to the trip into Bear Creek today and to a respite from Jack's vigorous lovemaking.

When he rolled out of bed at eight o'clock, a mere four hours after they had both fallen into an exhausted sleep, he had announced with irritating cheerfulness they would be spending the afternoon playing tourist. Thankfully, Jack and Marc had to deal with getting their guests checked out this morning and safely on their way, allowing her to roll over and sleep for another few hours. Morgan finished washing, wincing as she ran the soapy cloth between her legs, then forced herself to step out of the warm shower to dress and go in search of food.

"Are you ready?" Jack asked when he returned to the loft, noticing again how good she looked in a pair of jeans. *Down, boy*, he silently berated his cock when his first thought was how fast he could get them off of her. He had fucked her twice last night after they closed the club and he needed to give her a rest. Soon they would have to talk about her plans, something they had both avoided the last two days, but would need to address sooner rather than later. He knew she was everything he wanted, and he'd be more than happy to ask her to make a permanent move here, but she needed to be sure. She was young and inexperienced and could easily mistake lust for something deeper.

"I'm ready. Is Marc going?" she answered, grabbing her coat off a rack.

"He's pulling the Tahoe up front. He'll ride in with us, then meet us later for dinner. His errands will take him in a different direction, and right past the bakery, if I'm not mistaken."

"I'm surprised he doesn't gain weight, as much as he likes his sweets. I'd weigh as much as you if I indulged as often as he does," she commented as they went downstairs. It had taken every ounce of her willpower to resist the fat glazed donuts sitting on the kitchen counter the past two days.

"But I could help you burn those calories."

Morgan snorted. "Your type of exercise would leave me unable to walk, defeating the purpose."

"Don't worry, princess," he grinned, holding the door open for her. "I'd be sure to rotate between all your orifices so we didn't cause you any discomfort."

Morgan settled into the backseat, refusing to comment in front of Marc, although she was sure her red face gave away the gist of their conversation. The drive into Bear Creek took less than half the time it had taken her to reach the lodge due to the now cleared roads, and Morgan got a much better look at the scenery than she had through her snow-blocked windshield.

When Marc parked in front of a small, quaint store, Morgan could smell the enticing aromas coming from it as soon as she got out of the Tahoe. An elderly woman held the door open and greeted him by name.

"I'll catch up to you later," he called back as he hastened inside.

"That's Martha Harper, a widow who has a soft spot for Marc," Jack told her, clasping her hand and leading her down the cleared walkway.

"I could tell." Smiling, she tripped after him. The warm sun helped keep the cold air from numbing her face, and there was no wind, which made it a pleasant day to play tourist.

With fewer than five thousand residents, Bear Creek catered to tourists year round and Morgan fell in love with the small town atmosphere and neighbor-friendly citizens. Born and raised in Chicago with its crowded bustling activity, high crime rate, and constant noise, she could see the allure of this laidback existence, the main street with its one traffic light, quiet and peaceful, the business owners and residents friendly and open to strangers. Jack led her into small gift shops that sold goods native to Colorado, pointed out the hundred-year-old library and city building, made reservations for dinner at a restaurant boasting the best steaks and seafood outside of Denver, and then surprised her by directing her into a small art gallery.

"Jack, how are you?"

An attractive woman in her forties greeted Jack with a hug before turning her attention and beaming smile on Morgan. "And who's this?"

"Stephanie, this is Morgan, the artist I told you about." Jack almost laughed out loud at the astonished look on Morgan's face. "Morgan, Stephanie and her husband, James, own this gallery and sell the works of several local artists."

"I'd love to see some of your work. Jack tells us you're very talented."

After sending Jack a piqued look for putting her on the spot, she turned shy, saying, "I've only done a few sketches since I've been here and I left them at the lodge."

"I have them." Jack pulled out a few sheets he tore from her pad and tucked into his coat before they left. "You'll recognize these, Stephanie, drawn from our loft window."

"Oh, no, Jack, those aren't very good. I was just doodling." Embarrassed he'd show her inferior work, Morgan tried to grab them from his hand, but Stephanie already had a hold of them.

"Oh, my dear," she sighed, scanning the drawings. "If these are just doodling for you, I'd definitely like to see something you've put effort into. I could frame these and get forty dollars each for them easy."

"Huh?" Morgan looked at Stephanie as if she was out of her mind. "They're just charcoal sketches."

"Yes, but you've depicted the landscape with a perfect eye for detail and tourists would buy them as a souvenir of their trip and residents as a wonderful rendition of a favorite spot. Look around, dear, you'll see all kinds of different art from wood carvings, to sculptures, to paintings all of wildlife and scenery native to this area."

While Jack visited with Stephanie, Morgan looked around the small gallery, impressed with the talent she saw on display. Someone who loved wildlife had made beautiful wood sculptures of bears and their cubs, eagles with wings spread, and small raccoons resting on a log. Several framed paintings hung on the walls along with handmade quilts.

"When do you think you can get me some more sketches, or a painting?" Stephanie eagerly asked when she finished looking at all the different drawings.

"Oh, I appreciate the offer," Morgan stammered, not sure how to respond. Her life was currently in limbo until either Jack asked her to stay with him or she decided it was time to return to Chicago.

Taking her hand, Jack came to the rescue. "We'll let you know. Right now, Morgan has some unfinished business back home she needs to take care of before she can commit to anything."

"We charge twenty percent commission," Stephanie said, handing Morgan her card. "Stop by anytime you want, we'd love to display your work."

Flattered, Morgan took the card. "Thank you. It was nice to meet you."

Out on the sidewalk, Jack pulled her around to face him. "We need to talk, princess."

In a blinding flash of clarity, she looked up at him with

a goofy smile of sheer happiness. "You wouldn't have introduced me to Stephanie or brought those sketches if you wanted me to leave." It took a lot of nerve for her to dare him with that statement, but she wouldn't back down. She had chased after Jack her whole life and knew him well enough to keep her from backing down now, not unless he told her outright he wasn't interested in a permanent relationship with her.

"No, I wouldn't have, but you have to be sure. Not just about me, but about leaving your home, your job, everything you've known. And Morgan?"

His face and dark eyes were as serious as his tone, which made her quiver in uncertainty. The bright sunlight gilded his light hair, adding to the stark contrast with his dark beard, making him look even sexier. He was so big, she felt small and petite next to him and she wanted nothing more than to be with him always. It had been that way for her for twenty years. Not even his long absences could dissuade her from that desire. "What?" she asked, already knowing leaving her life in Chicago would pose no hardship.

"My lifestyle isn't a phase. When it comes to sex, I've shown you what I want, what I'll always demand as a lover."

Relieved, she teased him, saying, "And I think I've done a damn good job of showing you I not only accept your domination, but rather enjoy it."

He couldn't deny she had submitted to him as if she had been in the lifestyle for years, but it was hard to let go of the fears that had made him keep his distance for so long. But when had he ever been able to deny her anything?

Looking down into her bright eyes, he sighed in defeat. Kissing her nose, he said, "Can you stay a week or two longer without your parents sending the National Guard to rescue you from my evil intentions? After that, if you still want to move here, move in with me, well, there's nothing I'd like more."

Morgan went giddy with relief. He wanted to give a relationship with her a try, and that's all she's ever wanted.

"I have plenty of vacation time, but I don't need it. I know what I want, I've always known, Jack. As for my parents, they never gave a damn when I spent time with you before; in fact, I know they were grateful when I turned to pestering you for attention instead of them. I refuse to let them run my life now because they want something from me."

Draping his arm around her, he led them back down the street. "Try not to alienate them too much, Morgan. They are your parents."

"Well, it's a little late for them to remember that now."

Jack didn't blame her for being bitter, but he knew they wouldn't bow out without a fuss, not when they wanted something.

Their next stop was the garage repairing her car, and they were both pleased the side door was fixed and usable and the rest of the damage would be finished in a day or two. Morgan had instructed Jack to give the shop permission to make whatever necessary repairs were needed to get the BMW running again as she intended to trade it in for something more practical.

After meeting Marc for dinner, the three of them returned to the lodge where Jack left her alone in the loft while he and Marc went downstairs to put up the equipment and prepare the club room for the next couple of weeks of regular guests.

CHAPTER EIGHT

Two days later, Morgan sat in her favorite spot in front of the windows in the loft's great room, blissfully happy and more certain than ever life with Jack was what she wanted. With both guys busy preparing for new reservations, she spent most of her time drawing both from the window views and from various spots outdoors. She couldn't wait to get her paints from her apartment and start painting again. Her car had been delivered that morning and now she could make the trip back home to retrieve her things, but she was in no hurry. She definitely wasn't looking forward to the confrontation with her parents when she told them she was relocating permanently to Colorado. And she wasn't ready to leave Jack yet, not even for a few days. Not only would she miss him, but damn it, for the first time she had a satisfying sex life, and she didn't want to put it on hold, not even temporarily.

Jack's inventive expertise coupled with his stamina left her weak and trembling and eager for more. He took her whenever the mood struck, wherever they happened to be. She's gotten used to Marc walking in on them and her embarrassment never lasted long. This morning, when Jack bent her over the couch after breakfast, she wasn't even surprised when Marc had taken a seat behind them and jacked off while watching.

With the afternoon sun warming her, Morgan sketched the dainty doe and her fawn grazing at the tree line, trying to hurry before the pair disappeared into the woods. Engrossed in her thoughts, she didn't realize Jack had returned to the loft until his large, hard hands slid over her shoulders and down his shirt, the only thing she wore, startling her. Recognizing his touch, she leaned her head back and smiled up at him as he kneaded the full softness of her breasts. "Hi."

"Hi, yourself. This seems to be a favorite spot of yours," he said, referring to her place in front of the large windows.

"Mmm, yes, and your hands seem to have landed on a favorite spot of yours."

"Yes, they have. Your nipples were already hard though, which makes me wonder what you were thinking about." When she didn't respond, he gave each bud a tight pinch, drawing a moan from her. Her quick, eager responses never failed to surprise him and spur him on.

"I was thinking about this morning, and how good it felt to have you inside me," she gasped when he increased the pressure on her sensitive peaks.

Releasing her nipples, he resumed kneading her breasts. "And having Marc watch and get himself off? Did that excite you, princess?"

Squirming with embarrassed discomfort, she mumbled, "Maybe." It was one thing to enjoy having an audience and quite another to admit it.

"Does that mean you're not sure?"

Morgan glared up at him. "It means I don't want to talk about it. I'd rather have sex again."

"I don't like your tone, Morgan. I ask questions because I need to know how you feel. I especially need to know if there is something you're not comfortable with, and I need to know before you resent me for it."

She could tell by his cool tone he wasn't happy with her,

but she still found it difficult to admit certain things to herself, let alone him. "Yes, it turned me on to have him watch, is that what you wanted to hear?" she snapped.

"Only if it's the truth."

"What if I said I wasn't comfortable with what he did?"

Jack shrugged. "Then it wouldn't happen again." But now that he knew she was comfortable with Marc, they could take her a step further. Pulling away from her tempting, soft breasts, he held his hand out to her. "Come with me."

Clasping his hand, she followed him down the hall, her nipples stiff and tingling, her pussy damp and ready for his possession. When he led her into Marc's room instead of his, she looked at him in question. "What are we doing in here?"

Jack heard the unease in her voice and smiled at her. A little uncertainty was good, but he didn't want her afraid. "Marc has something I don't have in my room."

Following his look, Morgan saw the mirrored wall opposite the king-size bed. "Uh, Jack, I said I was okay with Marc watching us. That doesn't mean *I* want to watch." The thought of seeing her less than perfect body next to his left her unsettled.

"I do, and it's my wishes that matter. Strip and kneel facing the mirror, legs spread wide. I'll be right back."

His tone brooked no argument, which only seemed to turn her on more. Unbuttoning the shirt, she tossed it on the bed before going to her knees, keeping her eyes averted from her image in the mirror. When Jack returned carrying a round leather paddle and a small white tube, her nipples puckered even tighter and she could feel her copious juices seep from between her swollen lips, coating her thighs. Looking into the mirror, she watched Jack strip, her heart tripping as it always did at the sight of his thickly muscled body. When he knelt behind her, the hairs on his chest and legs tickled her, their rough abrasiveness exciting. Leaning back against him, she closed her eyes, moaning when his hands clasped her breasts.

"No, I want you to watch me pleasure you. Open your eyes," he demanded.

Morgan opened her eyes and watched him fondle her breasts, his hands dark against her lighter skin, his fingers grasping her nipples as his head dipped to the side to kiss her neck. Though she'd never cared to look at her naked body, right now she enjoyed the sight of his hands on her, loved the way he could arouse her within seconds of touching her, relished the way he knew her body and seemed to crave it as much as she did his.

"See how beautiful you are, Morgan? How your nipples respond to my touch?" Moving one hand in a slow, tantalizing caress down her waist, he palmed her pussy. "How wet you are, wet and swollen and eager for my cock." He slid his middle finger between her slick folds, enjoying the feel of her warm sheath and her increasing heartbeat beneath his other hand.

Thrusting into his hand, she begged, "Jack, please, quit tormenting me."

"Tsk, tsk. That's not the proper way to address me, now is it?" He shifted his hand from between her legs, around her hip, to palm her right buttock. "That's your second infraction. The first was your tone earlier. Turn sideways on your hands and knees. Now."

Morgan quivered as she moved into position, her breath snagging when he reached for the paddle and knelt behind her.

"Watch in the mirror while I paddle your pretty ass, Morgan."

She didn't want to, but she dared not disobey him when he used that tone. Turning her head, she winced as he brought the paddle down on her left buttock, cringing at the sight of her fleshy cheek. She cried out with the next swat, blossoming heat following the hot sting across her cheek, the burn going straight to her pussy. Another swat landed on her other cheek and then back to the left side. Slow and methodical, he alternated between soft and hard smacks, wringing gasps of pleasure/pain from her as he turned her entire backside into a mass of burning flesh. Lost in the throes of painful bliss, she closed her eyes, lifting her ass for each stroke even though she whimpered when it struck. With her concentration on her buttocks, on accepting the pain and the pleasure she got from it, she didn't notice Marc entering the room. It wasn't until she opened her eyes that she saw him standing in front of her, naked, his hard cock in his hand, his eyes watching Jack's ministrations.

"That's a beautiful sight, Jack," Marc said, his eyes shifting from her butt to her face as he smiled at her.

Morgan smiled back, grateful for his easygoing manner. When Jack set the paddle down and leaned over her back, his cock nestled between her sore cheeks, she welcomed the comfort of his embrace.

Kissing her neck, Jack whispered near her ear, "I want to watch you suck him while I take your ass. Will you do that for me?" Jack held his breath, waiting for her response. Her body stiffened at his request, but then relaxed, as if the idea held appeal. With a slight shift, he angled his cock down and caressed her folds, slipping between them to dampen his shaft, but not entering her. She was soaking, her breathing heavy, her nipples pebbled into points of arousal, all excellent signs of acceptance.

Turning to look at him, she whispered her uncertainty. "You won't mind?"

Chuckling, he kissed her. "Marc and I have shared women before, but I will admit, this won't happen often. I seem to be a bit possessive of you, princess."

Such a simple statement, but it went a long way toward reassuring her. Nodding her head, she turned back toward Marc, who watched her with calm patience, his cock hard and seeping.

"Open for me, darlin'." With his hand around the base of his shaft, Marc pushed between her soft lips and sank into the warm wet cavern of her mouth. "Shit, Jack, I won't last long."

"Then I better join you." Grabbing the tube of lubricant, Jack moved to kneel behind Morgan, her red buttocks an enticing lure. Coating two fingers, he spread her cheeks and pushed both digits into her tight hole in one stroke. Exploring her anus with slow, deep thrusts, he stroked along sensitive nerve endings while spreading a liberal coat of lubricant. Her low moan around Marc's cock and the telltale shift of her hips against him was all the encouragement he needed.

Morgan tried to concentrate on Marc's cock, but Jack's fingers delving between her buttocks made it difficult, more so when he pulled them back and replaced them with the slick head of his cock at her entrance. Bracing herself for his possession, she breathed a sigh of relief when he entered her with slow precision, his hands gripping her hips to keep her from moving and forcing too much of him at one time.

"Deep breaths through your nose, Morgan," Marc instructed her, his hands clasping her head to hold her still.

Held securely in front and back, Morgan could do nothing but take their cocks and glory in their possession. The invasion of Jack's cock in her ass burned, but the discomfort soon turned to pleasure, the plug experience and anal play he'd tormented her with helping make this first time easier. His slow possession stretched her to the point of pain, but by the time he filled her rectum with his full length, she found herself on the verge of climax.

Jack, whose attention didn't miss a thing, smiled and nodded at Marc. As the two of them sped up their thrusts, Jack slid his right hand between her legs and clasped her swollen clit between two fingers. "Come for us, princess. Come now." Milking her clit between his fingers as he pummeled her ass with his cock, her come soaked his hand, her cock-muffled scream music to both their ears.

Drowning in a sea of sensation, her ass spasming around Jack's cock, she came over and over, her mouth never releasing the treasure of Marc's plunging dick. When they joined her, she came again, her body shaking with the raw carnality of her release and their possession.

• • • • • • •

Morgan awoke to Jack's cock prodding her from behind, his body a warm and comforting embrace. "Are you ever satisfied?" she groaned.

"Relax, I'm not such a pervert as to take you so soon after what we put you through last night. Have I told you how fucking awesome you looked in the mirror with the two of us?"

"No, but thanks." She never tired of his compliments, never felt self-conscious around him because of them. It was only when she was away from his positive influence she still had doubts about herself. "So," she said, twisting around to snuggle up to his chest, watching his face closely. "Are you still mad I showed up here unannounced?"

Jack twisted her hair in his hand, using his grip to bring her face up to his. "You satisfy me so well it always leaves me wanting more. Maybe in fifty years I'll finally have my fill of you." His mouth took hers in a deep drugging kiss before he asked, "Does that answer your question?"

Giddy with delight at his answer, Morgan didn't think even fifty years would be enough for her. "Yes, thank you, Jack." Reaching down between them, she ran her nail lightly down his erection. "You know, I'm not sore *everywhere*."

"You could very well be the death of me, Morgan," Jack said on a long-suffering sigh before removing her hand. The slight sting from her nail had him seeping in pleasure, but he wasn't about to give in to her in this case. She needed to rest after the marathon of sex he'd put her through the past few days. With a laugh of pure contentment, he kissed her hard, swatted her ass, and jumped out of bed. Smiling at the way she rubbed her red cheek and glared at him, he warned, "You know what that look will get you."

"You sure know how to put a damper on my fun,

master," she retorted sarcastically. Pulling the covers up, she snuggled back down into bed. "You've had your fun, now go away."

The persistent peal of her phone woke her an hour later. Not fully awake, she grabbed the offending object off the nightstand and greeted the caller with a terse, "What?"

"Is that any way to answer your phone?"

Groaning, Morgan rolled over, sticking her head under the pillow. "What do you want, mother?"

"Are you ready to come home yet, Morgan?"

"What do I have to do to get it through your head I'm *not* marrying Joel? And, if I do come home, it'll only be to pack my things and return here. I want to be with Jack." Damn it, for once, why couldn't her parents be supportive?

"Then you leave me no choice. If you don't return home immediately and attend your engagement party Saturday night, your father will buy Jack's loan on that place and then call it in. He and his partner will lose everything."

"You wouldn't!" she gasped in outrage, jerking upright with trembling anger. Jack and Marc both loved this place and had worked hard to make it successful. There was no way she'd be responsible for them losing it.

"We would," Kathleen stated, her implacable tone coming through the phone clear as a bell. "Your father wants this merger, and since you're our only child, you've left us with no choice."

"So my happiness means nothing to you?" she whispered, feeling the crushing blow of defeat press down on her.

"Really, Morgan, must you be so melodramatic? You can have a perfectly nice life with Joel. After you give him a child or two, you can do as you please, as long as you're discreet. You can even spend your vacations in the mountains with Jack. After all we've done for you, you'd think you'd be grateful enough to repay us by helping out with this."

Morgan closed her eyes, wishing she could shut out her mother as easily. Her parents had always thought sending her to the best boarding school in the country, making sure she had gourmet meals and fancy clothes, was all a child needed. Thank God she had Jack and Agatha to show her someone cared about her, that she was worthy of love.

And because Jack meant everything to her, had been there for her when no one else had, she would not allow her parents to destroy his dream. She knew how hard he had worked and saved to buy this place. How could she bear it if she was the cause of him losing it? He would hate her if that happened, and that was the one thing she couldn't bear.

"I'll leave today, mother. Tell Joel I'll be there in time for the engagement party." Morgan hung up and then ran into the bathroom. Standing under the shower, she let the sobs come. She had been so close to having everything she had ever wanted. It was only with Jack she had ever been truly happy and when he had mentioned being together for fifty years this morning, she had thought her heart would burst. Now, her future looked so bleak, she didn't know how she could stand it. Jack would hate her after this; after pursuing him, practically throwing herself at him while assuring him it was what she wanted, he would never forgive her for turning away.

She couldn't do it, she thought, struggling to stem the flow of tears. She couldn't look into his face when she told him she was leaving without telling him why, and could never reveal her parents' threat, forcing him to choose between her and the lodge. That wouldn't be fair, and though she had often been selfish in her demands of him when she was growing up, she wasn't a neglected little girl any more, needing him to be there for her. This time, she needed to do what was right for him, no matter how much it hurt.

After drying off, she tried to cover the evidence of her tears with makeup and hoped Jack wouldn't notice. Dressed in jeans and a sweater, she swiftly stuffed her few belongings back in her bag, including Jack's flannel shirt she had lived in the past week. One week, that was all she had with him, all the happiness she would ever know. Of course, she had no intentions of staying with Joel permanently. After she produced the required heir, she would file for divorce. She may have lost Jack, but that didn't mean she would spend the rest of her life with that jerk. She'd raise her child with all the love she never had and hope someday she could tell Jack the truth and he would forgive her.

Leaving her bag until she could get away without being seen, she padded down the hall toward Jack and Marc's voices coming from the kitchen. Pausing to take a deep, fortifying breath and put on a fake face, she stepped into the great room on shaky legs.

"Well, look who finally woke up," Marc greeted her with a smile.

Morgan gave him her best smile, praying she fooled them as they each looked at her with worry. With hope, they'd put her reticence down to embarrassment over their threesome last night and not question her.

Jack noticed the change in Morgan as soon as he saw her. Since she was fine when he left the bedroom earlier, he could only surmise she felt uncomfortable around Marc. Remembering what happened between Marc and Cassie, he hoped he hadn't pushed her too far too fast. She had seemed to enjoy including Marc last night and had embraced the whole encounter with as much enthusiasm as she has everything else he introduced her to. Not that he intended to share her often. Maybe she needed to be reassured of that, and of his feelings for her.

"We saved you some banana pancakes. Come help yourself." Setting a plate in front of her as she took a seat at the counter, he then poured her a cup of coffee. "Marc and I have to go back to town to pick up supplies at the post office. Want to come?" He hoped having her accompany them with no sexual overtures would help put her at ease.

"No, thanks. I'd rather draw some more," she replied, thankful they were making her getaway easy. She needed to leave as soon as possible before she broke down and selfishly put her own happiness ahead of his.

"Morgan," Marc chided. "If you don't want me to go, I'll understand."

"No! I mean, that's not the reason. I really want to come up with some better sketches for Stephanie."

"Okay, if you're sure." Kissing her, Jack knew something was bothering her. Vowing he'd get it out of her when they returned, he said, "We won't be long."

Morgan listened to them joke as they went downstairs and knew she couldn't leave him without saying one more thing. Running to the balcony overlooking the lobby and foyer, she called down to him as he opened the front doors. "Jack, I love you."

He smiled up at her. "I know you do, princess. I love you too."

It wasn't the first time they had said those words to each other, but it was the first time they meant more than as a friend. She prayed it wasn't the last time she heard them.

• • • • • • •

Jack sat in the unlit club room and downed another whiskey. He and Marc had returned from Bear Creek by midafternoon and he'd known as soon as he'd stepped foot into the loft she was gone. A quick search had told him she hadn't left anything behind except a short note stating she had changed her mind and wanted to return home. His first thought had been to go after her, demand an explanation and that she give him another chance. But he hadn't been able to do it. He had only ever asked one thing of Morgan and that was for her to trust him. Apparently it was the one thing she hadn't been willing to give.

With a bleak stare at the empty room, he remembered how the little minx had been brave enough to sneak in and spy on the activities she was unaccustomed to seeing, brave enough to risk his wrath and punishment. And then, much to his surprise and pleasure, she had been brave enough to accept her punishment and embrace him and his lifestyle with all the enthusiasm she had always shown for new adventures, especially when they included him. In just a few short days he had put her through a sexual marathon, wasting no time introducing her to the pleasure/pain of sexual domination. And she had taken to each new experience with wholehearted enthusiasm, her multiple orgasms proof of her acceptance. So, why in the hell had she run instead of coming to him with her insecurities? Was it the threesome with Marc that sent her fleeing back home or was it something else? The only thing she had left him was a single sketch of his mountainside with her signature, that and heartache.

"I thought I'd find you here." Marc joined Jack at the bar.

"Sorry, Marc." Pouring another drink, he offered the bottle to him. "Care to join me or are you here to try to convince me I didn't fuck up?"

Taking the bottle, Marc capped it and put it out of his friend's reach. "You didn't fuck up, Jack. Think about it for a minute."

"You'd think we both would have learned our lesson with Cassie, wouldn't you?" Jack asked, his voice laced with sympathy because now he knew firsthand how Marc had felt this past year.

"What happened with Cassie wasn't the same. I screwed up big time with her and I admit it. I was so fucking obsessed I let that blind me to her youth and inexperience. Hell, Jack, I was an experienced dom assigned to a newbie. We had no relationship before I railroaded her into letting me top her on beginner's night, and the few nights after. When I wanted to share her with you, I didn't consider her innocence. I wanted that experience so bad for her, I never considered she would look at it as a betrayal. We both knew how easily new subs mistake their desire for submission as desire for just that dom. If you'd quit wallowing in self-pity, you'd see the difference."

"If it wasn't the sharing that made her leave, then what was it?" he demanded, having no clue why Morgan would take off without at least speaking to him first.

"That's what you need to figure out. Have you tried calling her?"

"No, and I'm not going to. I asked her to trust me, Marc, and she didn't. That girl isn't shy, not with me. You're right, we've known each other for twenty years, told each other everything, nothing was off limits. There is nothing she couldn't talk to me about, nothing we couldn't work out together. She chose not to and I refuse to chase after her like a lovesick puppy. This is exactly why I didn't want to cross that line from friendship to lovers," he finished with all the bitterness eating at him before downing his drink.

Marc's grin was rueful as he pointed out the obvious. "But you *are* a lovesick puppy."

"Fuck you."

"Nah, you're not my type." Sighing, Marc rose and returned the whiskey under the bar. "When you sober up, think about something. All her life, she's run to you, thrown herself at you, risking her heart in the process. If I were to guess, her leaving probably had something to do with protecting you rather than herself. Maybe, for once, you ought to be the one who runs to her."

Jack cleaned out his glass and then stumbled upstairs. Without bothering to change, he fell into bed and cursed when he automatically reached for her and she wasn't there. *God damn it.* Tomorrow, he would chase that girl down, demand an explanation, and then beat her ass for pulling this latest stunt.

• • • • • • •

The next evening, he was just finishing packing a bag for his flight the following morning, when his phone rang. Recognizing Agatha's number, he snatched it up, hoping she had news of Morgan. He had tried all day to call her, but she either wasn't answering or she had packed her phone where she couldn't grab it while driving. It took over fifteen hours to drive from Denver to Chicago, and now he had to worry about her being on the road alone, which just pissed him off more.

"Hello, Agatha."

"Jack, thank God I got hold of you. You've got to get here as soon as possible."

Agatha's frantic voice sent a chill through him. "Calm down and tell me what's wrong. Is Morgan all right?"

"All right?! She'll never be all right if she goes through with her parents' demands. That poor girl showed up here an hour ago looking exhausted, her eyes swollen from crying. And what did they do? They just said they were glad she came to her senses. I swear, those two are the coldest people I've ever met."

Jack paced, knowing from past experience he had to let Agatha vent before she could get to the point. "Agatha, do you know what's going on, why Morgan returned home without talking to me?"

"Of course I do. I held the poor girl while she sobbed her heart out and told me how they were blackmailing her into following through with this ridiculous sham of a marriage. They threatened to buy up your loan on your lodge and then call it in, ruining you. Poor dear, she couldn't bear it if they caused you to lose that place. And now they expect her to attend this engagement party tomorrow night as if everything was fine. You won't let our girl go through with this, will you, Jack?"

Jack cursed, wearily rubbing his face as he realized how easily this could have been avoided if Morgan had just come to him. The loan Marc and he had on the lodge and the surrounding acres was at a small bank, privately owned by another Army buddy of theirs and also a frequent visitor. There was no way Jeremy would sell him out.

"Of course not, but I want your word you won't let on to Morgan that I'm on my way there. She's going to face me and the consequences for not trusting me before I tell her that her parents' threat is futile. They can't hurt me."

CHAPTER NINE

Morgan snatched another glass of Champagne from the server as he walked by. Chicago's elite filled Kathleen and George Tomlinson's home, everyone there to celebrate her engagement to Joel Norris. The huge ballroom, which they usually kept closed off, echoed with the sounds of laughter and the melodious strains coming from the small orchestra in the corner. A sumptuous buffet ran the length of one wall while the opposite side of the room opened out onto the patio. The white marbled floor shone under the bright glitter of twinkling chandeliers. People mingled, smiled, danced, and congratulated her, and she was oblivious to it all.

Downing the full flute, she relished the burn and subsequent buzz as she forced herself to smile and pretend to be deliriously happy. Her parents kept close to her side for the first time in her life, and Joel made the effort to be seen with his arm around her or giving her a perfunctory kiss every so often before moving off to entertain himself with friends.

"Honestly, Morgan, must you drink like a commoner?" her father growled under his breath.

"Yes," she snapped back, "that is if you want me to get

through this charade without giving away what a farce it is."

"You always were an ungrateful child," he returned with cold disapproval.

"Spare me the lecture, father. I'm not in the mood to hear what loving and caring parents I have." She wanted nothing more than for this night to end so she could return to her apartment and wallow in grief.

A commotion at the front of the room caught their attention. Morgan watched wide-eyed as people parted and a tall, light-haired man strode with arrogant purpose into the room, his dark beard lending him a rough look. His worn jeans emphasized his thick, muscled thighs as he walked with slow, deliberate steps toward her, his dark eyes never leaving her face. Morgan's eyes filled with tears as the past twenty years ran through her head: her first sight of him when she was just seven years old and he fifteen; their reunions each summer when she returned from school; his patience with her as she followed him around all day and pestered him to entertain her; her heartache when he left for the Army and her joy when he returned; his anger when he caught her spying on him and his date; their first kiss; the arousal only he could sate.

Jack found her right away and his reaction came fast and hard. Wearing a hideous dress designed to hide her figure instead of flaunting it, she stood surrounded by people and had never looked so alone. Memories of the past assailed him: the lonely little girl who clung to him like a lifeline; the way she would exuberantly throw herself into his arms each time they were reunited; his exasperation in teaching her to drive; his concern when she cried when she hurt; the way he missed her when he left for the Army; the thirsty lust only she could slake. She watched him out of drenched whiskey eyes and his anger at her parents matched his anger at her for daring to throw away everything they had.

"Jack." Morgan had to physically fight back the urge to fling herself into his arms. It had only been two and a half days since she had seen him and she missed him more in that time than at any other time they were separated.

"Princess." Holding out his hand, he watched her with grave eyes. "I'm asking you one more time and one more time only. Trust me?"

Struggling to get past the sudden lump lodged in her throat, she realized Jack was throwing himself at her for the first time and there was no way she could turn away from him. In all the years she'd known him, he had only asked one thing of her. Praying she wasn't making a mistake they both would regret, she took his hand. "Yes."

"Then let's go." Jack pivoted to lead her away when Kathleen stepped in front of them.

"Morgan, this is a disgrace. If you do this, you know what we'll do."

"No, you won't," Jack stated, his voice dripping ice. Looking down into Morgan's worried face, he reassured her with a deliberate wink. "They can't touch our loan, Morgan, so don't pay any attention to their threats."

Relief filled her, making her giddy. Looking back at her mother, she smiled then leaned forward to give her a soft kiss on the cheek. "Goodbye, mother."

• • • • • • •

"How mad are you?" Morgan asked after he had pulled away from her parents' house. Though his face had softened when he looked at her with love in the ballroom, his profile now was rigid, his jaw clenched tightly.

"You could have avoided all this drama and saved us both a lot of trouble if you had just talked to me instead of running off, Morgan."

She really hated it when he spoke to her in that stiff, condescending tone, even though she deserved his anger. "You don't understand. They threatened to ruin you, buy your loan and then call it in. You and Marc would've lost everything," she protested, trying to defend herself.

Stopping at a red light, he swiveled to face her. "And had

you come to me and told me that, I could've told you our loan is held by a good buddy from the Army and a frequent guest at the lodge. Jeremy not only owns the small bank he manages, but he would never betray us that way. Your parents can't buy a loan that isn't for sale."

He made it sound so simple, but she recalled all too well the devastation her decision caused her. "How was I supposed to know that? I couldn't bear it if I caused you to lose the lodge. I know how much that place means to both you and Marc."

Jack reached over, grabbed her hand, and brought it to his lips. "Nothing means more to me than you, princess."

"Really?" she breathed, astonished. She knew he cared, but never realized how much.

The pleased smile she turned up made him smile in return, even though he was still angry with her. "Really, but you'll still have trouble sitting down tomorrow."

Not even that threat could diminish her happiness, and by the time he pulled up in front of a downtown hotel and opened the door for her, her pussy had creamed with anticipation. Jack remained silent until he ushered her into a suite on the fifth floor. She barely had time to appreciate the plush surroundings before he pulled her to him and crushed his mouth to hers. Morgan kissed him back, hungry to touch him, to feel him again, her tongue dueling with his, her moans filling his mouth. By the time he pulled back, she was desperate to have him inside her.

"Get out of that hideous dress."

He was still angry with her, but Morgan didn't blame him. With his dark eyes on her, she stripped the dress off and stood before him in thigh-high hose, heels, a thong, and a demibra.

"I don't want you to hide your body ever again, Morgan. Do you understand?"

"Yes," she agreed without hesitation. Right then, she'd agree to anything as long as he fucked her soon. God, she had missed him.

"You're awfully agreeable, princess. In a hurry for something?" His eyes softened with amusement when she clenched her fists at her side.

"I admit I made a mistake, Jack, and should have told you about my parents' threat instead of running out on you." Reaching up, she slipped open the first button on his shirt, giving him a teasing grin. "If you'll get naked, I'll make it up to you."

Jack took hold of her hands and stepped back. "As enticing as I find you like that, I want you naked. Strip and kneel face down on the bed."

Both nervous and excited about his dictate, she obeyed before he changed his mind. Her nipples beaded into two stiff points when she removed her bra and her arousal was more than evident in the dampness coating her bare folds when she slipped off her thong. Naked, she padded to the king-size bed, crawled into the middle and knelt down, her head on her arms, her ass toward him. For the first time in her life, she didn't feel self-conscious about her figure.

"Spread your legs wider."

His terse command added to her excitement and made her breath catch. Silence filled the room as she knelt there exposed, vulnerable, and open to him. She didn't realize she was holding her breath until she released it with a whoosh when she heard him remove his clothes. The bed dipped when he knelt behind her, and she relished the feel of his hard thighs next to hers as his arm came under her hips and lifted her butt. Though it wasn't unexpected, the first blow caught her unaware and made her cry out.

"Not too loud. We don't want security up here." Jack swatted her again, slapping her upraised ass hard, loving the bright red hue spreading over her delicate flesh. She was done pulling his strings and running roughshod over his emotions. She was his and she damn well better accept that and everything that meant, starting now. "You're coming back to Colorado with me first thing tomorrow."

"Yes, sir," she cried out as he smacked her again.

"You're going to live with me, sleep with me, and submit to me sexually." He followed up that dictate with three more hard swats.

"Yes, Jack, master, anything," she agreed as tears of pain, acceptance, and love slipped down her face. When his hand landed with controlled force between her legs, slapping her damp pussy, she screamed with the shocking pleasure/pain, spreading her knees further as she embraced his dominance over her.

Jack slapped her pussy again and then again, holding her hips elevated as she kept her knees spread. When her soft folds were pink and warm, he moved back to her buttocks, his hand descending with calculated swiftness until she was sobbing and begging him to fuck her.

Morgan's ass throbbed in hot, puffy soreness by the time Jack relented and lowered her hips. She moaned, shuddering when he rubbed the flesh he had just abused, his soft strokes arousing her to a fevered pitch. When his fingers slipped down to caress her pussy then slid into her, she damn near came.

"No, Morgan," Jack said harshly as he fucked her wet sheath with three fingers. "No orgasm for you yet." Pulling out of her, he chuckled when she clamped around him, trying to hold his fingers inside of her. Without pause, he lifted her hips again and thrust his slick coated fingers into her ass, fingering her with ruthless, deep strokes. His cock hardened further at the sight of his fingers buried in her ass as he held her up for his use. Her soft mewling cries and the way she pushed back against him showed her acceptance and pleasure. "Does that feel good, baby?" he asked, his voice hoarse with lust, needing to hear the words as he thrust in and out of her anus, stretching her, preparing her for his possession.

"God, yes, master, so good. Please, fuck me. I can't bear it any longer." Her pussy wept with emptiness and need as he stretched her ass, teasing sensitive nerve endings beyond endurance and forcing her to hold back her climax. She needed him inside her first, needed to feel his possession of her before she succumbed to the pleasure. He made her wait though as he continued finger-fucking her ass until she writhed in his tight hold and begged for release.

Jack pulled out of her and grabbed the lube, liberally coating his cock before kneeling behind her, spreading her warm, red cheeks and thrusting into her prepared hole.

"Now, Morgan," he demanded on a harsh breath, slipping one hand beneath her to tease her clit. "Come for me, now."

Morgan could do nothing but obey as he took her ass with hard, deep strokes while his fingers milked her clit. Her hips met each thrust with trust as she bore down against his hand, adding pressure to her clit. Her climax burst upon her with the speed and heat of a firecracker, colors exploding behind her closed eyes as the wicked pleasure took over her senses, leaving her unaware of anything except the hard cock in her ass and the hard fingers clasping her clit.

Jack couldn't hold back after feeling her release coating his hand and the tight clench of her ass around his cock. With a few more deep strokes, he came inside her, filling her with his seed and finally claiming her for his own.

THE END

STORMY NIGHT PUBLICATIONS WOULD LIKE TO THANK YOU FOR YOUR INTEREST IN OUR BOOKS.

If you liked this book (or even if you didn't), we would really appreciate you leaving a review on the site where you purchased it. Reviews provide useful feedback for us and for our authors, and this feedback (both positive comments and constructive criticism) allows us to work even harder to make sure we provide the content our customers want to read.

If you would like to check out more books from Stormy Night Publications, if you want to learn more about our company, or if you would like to join our mailing list, please visit our website at:

www.stormynightpublications.com

Manufactured by Amazon.ca
Bolton, ON